Santi had come here to secure the advice l also to right a wrong.

Several wrongs in fact, because he was not some plaything of the rich to be picked up and discarded at will like his mother. He was not Thalia's inferior, despite what she'd intimated shortly before turning her back on him and walking out of that Paris hotel room. And no one rejected him these days.

Closure was what he wanted. Retribution. And to that end he intended to decimate her objections to him and rekindle their affair. To reel her in slowly and surely, to finish what they'd started. When the time was right, when the attraction had faded and he was ready, he'd let *her* go. And then, with the record set straight, the bewilderment and humiliation all hers, the power and invincibility once again all his, he'd finally be able to move on.

Lucy King spent her adolescence lost in the glamorous and exciting world of Harlequin when she really ought to have been paying attention to her teachers. But as she couldn't live in a dreamworld forever, she eventually acquired a degree in languages and an eclectic collection of jobs. After a decade in southwest Spain, Lucy now lives with her young family in Wiltshire, England. When not writing or trying to think up new and innovative things to do with mince, she spends her time reading, failing to finish cryptic crosswords and dreaming of the golden beaches of Andalucia.

Books by Lucy King

Harlequin Presents

Stranded with My Forbidden Billionaire

Heirs to a Greek Empire

Virgin's Night with the Greek
A Christmas Consequence for the Greek

Lost Sons of Argentina

The Secrets She Must Tell
Invitation from the Venetian Billionaire
The Billionaire without Rules

Passionately Ever After...

Undone by Her Ultra-Rich Boss

Passion in Paradise

A Scandal Made in London

Visit the Author Profile page
at Harlequin.com for more titles.

The Flaw in His Rio Revenge

LUCY KING

HARLEQUIN
PRESENTS

Recycling programs
for this product may
not exist in your area.

ISBN-13: 978-1-335-59349-8

The Flaw in His Rio Revenge

Copyright © 2024 by Lucy King

For questions and comments about the quality of this book,
please contact us at CustomerService@Harlequin.com.

TM and ® are trademarks of Harlequin Enterprises ULC.

Harlequin Enterprises ULC
22 Adelaide St. West, 41st Floor
Toronto, Ontario M5H 4E3, Canada
www.Harlequin.com

Printed in Lithuania

MIX
Paper | Supporting
responsible forestry
FSC® C021394

The Flaw in His Rio Revenge

CHAPTER ONE

AT ELEVEN P.M. on a Saturday night in September, in the gilded ballroom of a seven-star Athens hotel, the charity auction at the Stanhope Kallis Foundation gala was drawing to a close. A sumptuous six-course dinner accompanied by the finest wines had preceded it, and as a result, over the last hour, millions of euros had been thrown at luxury villas, questionable art and cases of claret by well-fed, well-oiled guests determined to outdo each other.

Santiago Ferreira, however, who was lounging in the seat for which he'd paid a five-figure sum, had eaten little, drunk less and was saving his money for the last lot on the list.

Stone-cold sober, biding his time and ignoring the puerile one-upmanship that was going on around him, he slowly turned his coffee this way and that. He watched as up on the stage Thalia Stanhope, the foundation's CEO, hovered in the wings. Her dark hair was swept up into an elegant pile on the top of her head. The pearls dangling from her earlobes and circling her throat gleamed white against her olive skin. The full-length dress encasing her pneumatic body was cherry-red and tight.

She was more beautiful than he remembered, he thought, letting his gaze drift over her dispassionately. So cool and composed, despite the sultry sensuality. She—the daughter of an aristocratic British banking mogul and a Greek shipping socialite, who'd been brought up with immense privilege and educated at the world's finest institutions—was the epitome of class, sophistication and inherited wealth.

He, on the other hand, was the now-orphan son of an impoverished single mother and a wealthy father who'd refused to acknowledge him—and whom he'd therefore never met—and had grown up in a shack in a drugs-and-guns-ridden favela on the outskirts of Rio de Janeiro. He'd received very little in the way of formal education and hadn't even learned to read and write until he was fourteen. He was brash not subtle, rough not elegant, and *his* wealth was newly acquired.

He was everything she wasn't, as she'd once so brutally reminded him. But that hadn't stopped them embarking on a blazing affair the evening they'd met on Naxos, at the wedding of a former colleague of his to Thalia's twin brother, sixteen months ago. One look across the bar was all it had taken to detonate an explosion of heat between them and instinctively propel him towards her, even though his mother's experiences of the rich and privileged had taught him that getting involved with someone like her would be madness.

'Dance with me,' he'd murmured, in the faintly accented yet flawless English he'd vowed to master the minute he'd realised it was the language of technology.

'Yes,' she'd replied breathlessly, her English polished to perfection by a Swiss finishing school that had been followed by Oxford.

He could recall nothing of the music they'd swayed to. Nothing of their surroundings. All he'd been aware of was the soft warmth of her body pressed up against his, the thundering of his pulse and the dizzying wildness of their kisses. Later, they'd tumbled into bed, setting fire to the sheets until dawn, and had subsequently met up whenever they were on the same continent at the same time, which, as the weeks had gone by, had occurred with increasing frequency.

Any misgivings had been dazzled into submission. That cool, cultured exterior of hers had concealed a volcano of passion the likes of which he'd never encountered before, all the more mind-blowing for its unexpectedness. And she'd seemed equally hooked on him. The minute the door to whichever hotel room they'd booked closed, she'd cast off her reserve, along with her clothes, and she'd launch herself at him, overwhelming him with a scorching blast of passion and need that without fail took out his knees and obliterated his brain. Their chemistry had been off the scale, their desire for each other insatiable. Their X-rated video calls had been so blisteringly hot it had always surprised him afterwards that their devices hadn't incinerated.

And then, twelve weeks later, thirteen months ago, she'd ended it. She'd just told him one day that they needed to talk—which, as everyone knew, meant only one thing—and once they were done, she'd coolly picked up her things and left. Which had never happened to him before because *he* was the one to terminate a relationship. *He* was the one who called the shots. Always. He *never* checked his phone for missed calls and messages that didn't come. He never *dwelt*. He moved on with no looking back and zero regrets.

That was why the abrupt end to their affair still irritated him so much, like a splinter lodged so deep it couldn't be prised out. Why it still dogged his thoughts day and night. Why he was stuck, unable to move on. He had not been ready to let her go. He'd been caught off guard. Humiliated. Stunned by the icy hauteur he'd never encountered in her before. She'd robbed him of his control and his strength and riddled him with doubt and confusion for the first time in years.

This disruption to his personal life could not be allowed to continue, he'd realised after months of wallowing in bitterness and self-pity. It had gone on for far too long already and enough was enough. Where he came from, weakness and uncertainty could get you killed. Obsession with the opposite sex, he learned at an early age, led to powerlessness, misery and despair. An absence of control could easily lead to unwise decision-making and impulsivity.

And so he'd come here tonight. Not just to secure the advice he sought but also to right a wrong. Several wrongs in fact, because he was not some plaything of the rich, to be picked up and discarded on a whim like his mother. He was not Thalia's inferior, despite what she'd intimated shortly before turning her back on him and walking out of that Paris hotel room. And no one rejected him these days.

Closure was what he wanted. Retribution. And to that end he intended to decimate her objections to him and rekindle their affair. To reel her in slowly and surely and to finish what they'd started. When the time was right, when the attraction had faded and he was ready, he'd let *her* go. And then, with the record set straight, the bewilderment and humiliation all hers, the power and invincibility once again all his, he'd finally be able to move on.

It was a simple but effective plan. He didn't doubt it would work. He was exceptionally single-minded and could be very persuasive when he chose to be. He'd had to put things on hold in order to focus on the recent sale of his software business, but that had been finalised and signed off six weeks ago. Having been catapulted from millionaire to billionaire, he now had a bank balance to rival hers, and all the time in the world to pursue other objectives.

'And lastly, to our final lot,' intoned the auctioneer, as every muscle Santi possessed tightened and adrenalin surged through his system. 'If you want to set up a foundation, expand your charity or organise a fundraiser and need a little help, this one's for you. Our CEO, Thalia Stanhope, is offering one hundred hours of her valuable time to consult and advise on any aspect of your enterprise. With a decade of experience in the sector, what she doesn't know isn't worth knowing. She is the ultimate expert. The best in the business. Who'll start me at fifty thousand?'

Silver paddles started flashing up and down almost instantly and within minutes the price for the lot had reached a quarter of a million.

Who'd have thought there'd be so much charitable feeling in the room? Santi reflected wryly, impervious to the growing buzz, his pulse beating steadily as the bidding continued apace, but pointlessly. Or was it the idea of spending one hundred hours in Thalia's company that was so appealing? He could understand that, on a superficial level. It had been double that amount of time before she'd shown him her true colours. Six weeks into their affair, he'd still been in her thrall, completely taken in by her exquisite façade and fiery passion.

But the motives of others were irrelevant. No one was going to win her but him, and his rivals had had their fun. It was time to close this lot down and activate the plan.

'Fifty million euros,' he said in an uncompromising tone that cut through the proceedings and warned everyone else to back the hell off.

A stunned silence descended over room, then the auctioneer found his voice and a minute later, with the bang of the gavel and a rush of triumphant satisfaction that was unexpectedly intense, given the fact that the outcome of the lot had never been in any doubt, Thalia was his.

CHAPTER TWO

FIFTY MILLION EUROS? What on earth was Santi Ferreira playing at? Who paid five hundred thousand euros an hour for *advice*? Why would he even want to? Was he *mad*?

Suppressing her shock and stamping out a sharp flare of emotion, Thalia somehow managed to deliver her speech, thanking everyone for their donations and support. Then she coolly stepped off the stage as if she hadn't just experienced an upset of cataclysmic proportions.

So much for assuming his presence here this evening was a benign coincidence, she thought darkly, as she batted aside a claim for her attention and made a beeline for him instead, no longer remotely interested in keeping her distance but intent now on finding out what he was up to.

Despite the attendance of six hundred guests, she'd clocked him the minute he'd walked in. With his towering height, powerful build and knee-trembling looks, he didn't exactly blend in. But even though she'd been irritatingly aware of where he was and who he was speaking to virtually every single second of every single minute, she'd steered well clear. The last time they'd seen each other had not been pretty, and she'd had zero desire to make an approach. Neither had he, she'd assumed with increasing relief as the time had passed without contact. But clearly she'd been labouring under a false sense of security. Because, since one presumably didn't spend fifty million euros in the heat of the moment, he must have had this move up his sleeve all along.

Behind her, up on the stage, a swing band consisting of ten sharp-suited musicians with vintage instruments got going, but all her attention was focused on the man who'd upturned her evening so dramatically.

With every inch of progress towards him her heart thudded faster and the odd fluttering in her stomach intensified. There were so many unknowns to the situation she thought, her nerves twisting tighter. She was at such a disadvantage. She'd have to establish control right from the off and set him straight on a few things because, whatever the reasons behind his winning bid, she couldn't work with him. She just couldn't. He was too overwhelming, too much of a distraction, too *everything*. That was why she'd had to end their affair all those months ago, even though it had been the last thing she'd wanted to do.

She could recall the moment they'd met as if it were yesterday. Her twin brother's wedding had been an event that, to her shame, she'd been dreading, and it had turned out to be every bit as difficult as she'd anticipated. She'd been sitting at the bar, nursing a glass of ouzo and struggling to untangle her complicated feelings about Atticus marrying Zoe—and killing off their ultra-close thirty-year twinship for good—when some sixth sense had prickled her skin and tightened her chest.

Her mouth dry, her pulse pounding in the most peculiar way, she'd looked up and around, and there he had been. The best looking, sexiest man she'd ever laid eyes on staring at her from the other end of the bar. Tall, broad-shouldered, his shaggy sun-streaked hair tousled as if he'd just rolled out of bed. And his eyes... Somehow, they'd seemed to smoulder. Dark and intense, they'd fixed on hers so intently that, for one long heart-stopping moment, she hadn't been able to breathe, let alone look away.

The guests, the music, her turbulent feelings, everything else had simply dissolved. All she'd been able to see was him. All she'd been able to hear was the thundering of her blood in her ears. Then he'd lowered his glass, his mouth curving into one slow devastating smile of pure temptation, and the burst of heat that had swept through her body had nearly burned her to a crisp where she sat.

This man could be exactly what she needed, she'd thought dazedly, desire pummelling away inside her as he'd headed in her direction, his compelling gaze unwavering, his intentions thrillingly obvious. A delicious distraction. A gorgeous, sexy pick-me-up who could grant her the oblivion she craved.

And that night he'd been everything she'd hoped for. In his arms on the dance floor everything but the feel of his hard body plastered against hers and his intoxicatingly masculine scent had fled her head. Afterwards, up in her room, he'd made her forget her own name so skilfully and so often that when he had enquired about her schedule and they'd discovered that they would both be in Italy the following week, she hadn't thought twice about agreeing to his suggestion that they meet up again.

For three giddy months she'd indulged the insane chemistry that burned between them, thinking about him constantly, almost to the point of obsession, until the voice in her head became too loud and insistent to ignore any longer. How could she figure out who she was without her twin brother if she didn't allow herself the time and the headspace to work on it? it persisted. How could she learn to forge her own path in life if she remained tangled up with someone else?

Atticus was the only person in this world who'd ever truly understood her, who'd been there for her no matter what. She'd always had him to turn to and rely on. Together, they'd survived the childhood trauma of appallingly neglectful parenting. But now she had to discover how to stand on her own two feet. And that couldn't happen if she kept falling back on Santi, who had swept her off into a different world, where she didn't have to think about anything but them every time they met.

Deep down she'd known that terminating their fling was the right thing to do, but the thought of it had nevertheless kept her awake at night and nauseated her by day. Having to explain to him the reason for doing so when she could barely articulate it herself had tightened the knots in her stomach even further. But in the end, with his shockingly unexpected and profoundly hurtful accusations of arrogance and snobbery in response to her announcement that they needed to talk, he'd made it very easy for her.

Thalia's heart thudded frantically as she neared and Santi rose from the seat in which he'd been lounging so carelessly, all gorgeously untamed six foot three inches of him clad in a perfectly fitting black dinner suit. His eyes were locked onto hers. A lazy smile played at his beautiful mouth. He wore his hair shorter now, she noticed distractedly. She thought she preferred it longer, even though the newly exposed cowlick was quirkily attractive. Then he slowly tugged free his bow tie and undid the top two buttons of his snowy white dress shirt, revealing a tantalising wedge of tanned skin, and a torrent of memories that she'd fought so hard to erase cascaded into her head. Of her undressing him. Of him undressing her. And then the touching and the heat and the uncontrollable need...

A burst of bittersweet longing swept through her and she was filled with the clamouring urge to grab his hand and haul him off upstairs, into the nearest available bedroom, in order to establish just how reliable her memories were.

But that was not going to happen, she told herself, ruthlessly obliterating the unwelcome desire and straightening her spine. Their bridges were well and truly burned and she was making great progress on her journey of self-discovery. She was successfully navigating solo relationships with her scandalous, self-centred mother and her four other siblings. Career-wise, she was breaking free from the safety net of the foundation and branching out on her own. She was being brave and taking risks and she would allow absolutely nothing to jeopardise any of it.

'Good evening,' he said in sexily accented English, his deep voice skating over her nerve endings, sending shivers down her spine and, appallingly, tightening her nipples.

It wasn't a good evening at all, she thought, gritting her teeth against the unwanted response of her body to his, hugely grateful for the thick fabric of her dress that concealed the evidence. In fact, thanks to him, it was quite possibly the most stressful evening she'd had in months and, given the emotional rollercoaster of the last year, that was saying something.

'That's debatable,' she said with a cool smile, drawing on the diplomatic skills she'd picked up at finishing school, designed to hide all true thoughts and feelings. 'But fifty million euros is quite a sum. It will be appreciated by many.'

'You're welcome.'

'However, it does come as something of a surprise.'

His dark eyes glinted with—what was that? Triumph?—and a strange sense of wariness rippled through her. 'It's been a long time.'

One year, four weeks and three days. Not that she'd been counting. 'It has indeed.'

'How have you been?'

There was a question. In the aftermath of their breakup she'd been a hurt, soggy mess—for longer than she cared to acknowledge. Having eventually got over him, she'd then had to deal with the fallout of her brother's marriage, which had been, and still was, very emotional and stressful. Now, tonight, she wasn't quite sure how she was. Unsettled, baffled and faintly dizzy from the effects of his head-spinning scent might just about cover it.

'Couldn't be better,' she lied smoothly, wishing the band weren't quite so loud, so they didn't have to be standing quite so close. 'You?'

'Exceptionally well.'

'I'm so pleased.'

'You've been avoiding me all evening.'

He'd noticed? How? Had he been as aware of her as she had of him? Surely pique couldn't be the reason for his outrageous bid. 'If you wanted my attention, Santi, all you had to do was call.'

'Would you have picked up the phone?'

She would have last August. For days after they'd parted company in Paris she'd waited for an apology that had never come. It was mortifying to recall how pathetically weak she'd been when the whole point of splitting up had been so she could find her inner strength. 'I guess we'll never know.'

'Would you like a drink?'

'No, thank you.'

'Then let's dance.'

As the memory of what had happened the last time they'd hit the dance floor flashed through her head, her heart skipped a beat and then began to race. 'Absolutely not,' she said, determinedly not thinking about the hot, wild kisses that had practically blown the top of her head off that night.

'For old times' sake.'

A shudder ran through her. 'I see no need to re-call those.'

'What are you afraid of?'

Nothing she was going to admit to him. It pained her to admit to herself how strongly he still appeared to affect her. 'Tripping over my dress.'

'I won't let that happen.'

He planted a hand at the base of her spine, his touch burning her like a brand. But even though she nearly jumped out of her skin with shock, and every instinct urged her to pull away, she did not. She would not let him see what he was doing to her. Nor would she cause a scene. They were attracting enough attention as it was. So she pulled herself together and went with him to the dance floor. And when he took her hand in his, his arm around her waist to hold her close, she did not think about how much she'd missed the heat and strength of his body or the feel of his skin against hers.

'So let's talk terms,' he said, beginning to move her skilfully around the space, while she resisted the temptation to stare at his mouth or tuck her head into the perfectly positioned spot where his neck met his shoulder and assured herself that this torture couldn't last for long.

'Do you really want my advice?'

'What else would I want?'

'I have no idea.' That was the trouble. He was as unreadable as a blank page and she couldn't work out quite what was going on. 'But we have history and you paid well over the odds for my time.'

He tutted. 'So suspicious.'

'Can you blame me?'

'Not for that.'

Thalia frowned. What was he talking about? What else could he blame her for? If anyone had the right to be aggrieved it was her. He was the one who'd been brutal when she'd hoped they'd be able to part as friends. 'I'm not sure I follow.'

'I sold my business.'

'So I read. In a record-breaking deal. Congratulations.'

'Thank you.'

'You must be very proud.'

Something unidentifiable flickered in the depths of his dark gaze. 'It's just money,' he said with a faint shrug of the muscled shoulder she had a hand on.

'It's a lot of money. In fact, you might now be even richer than me.'

'Quite possibly. We'll have to compare bank balances some time.'

Hmm. 'So what are you going to do with it?'

'I intend to channel a significant chunk into philanthropy. However, I have no idea how to go about doing that, and even less inclination to devote hours to finding out, hence my need for your expertise.'

'I'm flattered.'

'I hear you're the best in the business.'

She was.

Or at least she'd thought she was.

She'd worked for the sixty-year-old family foundation for a decade, helping it to fulfil its mission to improve the lives of millions of people around the world. It tackled complex social problems, established educational and health programmes and supported entrepreneurial and empowerment initiatives. It built communities and changed outcomes.

Joining the organisation straight from university, Thalia had thrown herself into the work. She'd started at the bottom, learning from the ground up, and had been appointed CEO five years ago. In this position, she oversaw fundraising ventures and the allocation of those funds.

She'd loved every minute of all of it.

Until recently.

She'd always known that her surname and the status it inferred had fast-tracked her career. Her connections were unparalleled, her wealth unimaginable. Because of who she was—a member of the glamorous Stanhope Kallis clan—she was invited to the most prestigious events and had access to the richest, most beneficent people in the world. She'd never minded that. With privilege came responsibility, she'd always felt.

But ever since Atticus had met Zoe, and she'd had to reassess her life, it had begun to bother her. Was she genuinely good at what she did or was she merely a convenient figurehead? Did she command real respect or was she just being indulged? As the doubts had settled in she'd begun to question every decision she'd ever made and every conversation with the board she'd ever had, until she'd no longer been certain of anything.

The morning of the eleventh day in a row that she'd woken up dreading going into work she'd decided that the only way to find out what she was truly capable of was to take the plunge and branch out on her own. Setting up a consultancy service to provide charitable advice and support to others might backfire but, on the other hand, it might not. She'd never know if she didn't try. And that was what her lot this evening had been about—not just to raise money for good causes but also to land a high-profile client with whom she could launch her new business with a bang.

Well, she'd certainly achieved that, she thought as Santi twirled her out, round and back into him again. Right now, with his mega-bucks deal still reverberating through the business world, he was as high-profile as they came. If they hadn't had a past he'd have been the ideal candidate. So she had to ignore her misgivings and get a grip. What she was trying to achieve both personally and professionally was too important to be scuppered by a handful of historic hurt feelings and irritatingly persistent chemistry. She had to be mature and rational about this, because it sounded as though he did genuinely need her help, and a deal was a deal.

'I'll set up a call,' she said, accepting the fait accompli with as much grace as she could muster. 'Does this coming Wednesday suit?'

'This coming Wednesday doesn't suit at all.'

'What about the following week?'

'I'd prefer to conduct our discussions face to face,' he said, his cool smile hinting at implacability. 'With maximum privacy and minimal distraction.'

How irritating. 'My office here in Athens, then.'

'Or my home in Brazil, on the coast, west of Rio. I was thinking ten days, ten hours a day, eight to six.'

Outwardly, Thalia continued to move with him in time to the music, but inwardly she reeled. He wanted her to fly halfway across to the world to stay with him in his house for ten days? What on earth was he *thinking*? Had he completely lost his mind? On no level was it a good idea. It was unnecessary, unprofessional, unacceptable, and absolutely not going to happen. 'I'm afraid that won't be possible.'

'Why not?'

Because she didn't want to spend time with him and remember how badly he'd hurt her and how naïve and stupid he'd made her feel. Because awkwardness and tension did very much not make for an atmosphere conducive to working together. Because containing the unfortunate attraction she apparently still felt for him would be a herculean battle, and she wasn't a masochist.

And what if it got too much and she failed to resist him? The potential for mortification didn't bear thinking about. The implications of a relapse and undoing all the progress she'd made appealed even less. 'I have commitments.'

'Rearrange them.'

'As I'm sure you'll appreciate, it's not that easy.'

'Fifty million euros says it is.'

At that, she visibly stiffened. Goosebumps broke out all over her skin and her blood chilled. For a moment all she could do was stare at him in shock, frozen rigid in his arms, thinking, who was this man with his diktats and blackmail and his relentless attempts to crush her arguments to dust? Had she ever known him at all?

'Are you suggesting that if I refuse to accommodate your demands, you'll withdraw your donation?' she said, once she'd regained the power of speech.

'Would you like to put it to the test?'

No, she would not. The foundation welcomed every cent it was promised and she could not deny it such a fortune. And much as she might loathe the idea, she needed him. Reneging on the deal that had just been struck would damage her reputation for trustworthiness and reliability, and where else was she going to find a client of his calibre? Those who'd been bidding for her lot before he'd swooped in to snatch her up didn't come close.

She had no option but to yield to his outrageous terms. And it would be fine. She could bury the attraction. She'd just have to. From here on in, she'd channel indestructible resilience and Sphynx-like serenity. However deep she had to dig, whatever the provocation, she would remain cool and composed. She would battle every further attempt he made to wrestle control from her. She'd once given it up all too willingly, and she would not be that careless again.

She'd resist his charms and ignore the unwelcome effect he had on her. She'd look forward, not back.

After all, theirs would be a professional relationship, and with his ten ten-hour days, a finite one at that. She would not fail. He would never know how much he'd hurt her with his cruel accusations. How devastated she'd been to discover how little he'd thought of her, when she'd thought the world of him. He'd certainly never know that he continued to have such a dramatic impact on her, despite her desperately wishing otherwise. So she lifted her chin and pulled her shoulders back and said, 'Of course not.'

'Because I'm sure there are others out there who'd welcome the opportunity to work with me.'

Well, *that* wasn't happening. 'But none with my experience and expertise.'

'Excellent,' he said with an annoying air of smug satisfaction. 'Then we're agreed. I'll see you at the airport, tomorrow morning at nine.'

CHAPTER THREE

The reason Santi had boarded the plane at seven thirty this morning, a whole ninety minutes before he had arranged to meet Thalia, was because even though his body clock, still on Brazil time, should have switched him off like a light, he'd had a fitful night, thanks to unexpectedly erotic dreams in which she had had a starring role, and eventually he'd figured that he might as well head to the airport and kick up his heels there instead of in his hotel room. It had nothing whatsoever to do with the habit he'd once developed of turning up early at whichever venue they'd agreed upon so he could enjoy the anticipation of her arrival. Similarly, he'd taken up his current position—horizontally sprawled along the sofa—in order to relax and enjoy the buzz of owning a brand-new top-of-the-range plane. The fact that it afforded him a view of the door was mere coincidence.

Everything was going exactly according to plan, he thought with bone-deep contentment, as he took another quick glance at his watch, the third in as many minutes. The only thing he hadn't considered was the physical impact Thalia apparently still had on him.

Last night, he'd watched her make her approach and his pulse rate had rocketed with every step she'd taken. It was in the expectation of the righting of wrongs, he'd told himself, easing the sudden pressure on his windpipe by loosening his bow tie and unbuttoning his collar. Although that hadn't explained the lightning strike of heat that had shot through him so unexpectedly that he'd nearly forgotten where they were and everything that had happened, and pulled her in for a kiss.

Instead, he'd opted for a dance, to remind her of how hot they'd been together. He hadn't expected to remember how perfectly she fitted him or how in synch they moved. And he certainly hadn't anticipated responding to her quite so powerfully, until he'd forced himself to recall what this was all about so he could refocus. But intense chemistry was hardly a problem. On the contrary, it would make the job of seducing her into his bed when the time came quite literally a pleasure.

A shift in the air and a tingling of his skin indicated Thalia's embarkation, and a moment later she entered the cabin. This morning she was wearing a navy trouser suit over a white shirt. Her dark glossy hair was tied up and back, but her effect was no less potent now than it had been the night before. When her gaze landed on him, slowly travelling from his bare feet up the length of his body to the top of his head, it left a scorching trail of fire in its wake.

'Good morning,' he said gruffly, ablaze yet unable to tell from her inscrutable expression whether her perusal of him had affected her in any way. Not that it mattered particularly. Her frosty demeanour last night suggested that, for her, the attraction had dimmed—but he'd soon relight it. Combustible chemistry like theirs didn't disappear completely. All he had to do was switch on the charm and let nature take its course.

'Nice plane,' she said, smoothly turning her attention to the well-appointed space as she advanced into it.

'Thank you.'

'Yours?'

'As of a month ago, yes.'

'It's immaculate.'

The wood was polished to a gleam he could see his reflection in. The carpet was thick, cream coloured and unmarked. It was everything he'd specified, far surpassing his expectations, and the first time he'd flown in it, he'd thought, *Not bad for a kid from the favela.*

'It's brand new.'

'Ours could do with an upgrade.'

'How many do you have?'

'The company has three. The family has one, which is usually commandeered by my mother. All of them are ancient and none of them is the size of this.'

'This is the biggest there is.'

'Naturally,' she said with a dryness that made him frown briefly, because what was she implying? That new money bought the shiniest and best while old made do and mended? Well, so what if it did? At least he'd earned his billions. In his view, it was those who hadn't who merited derision.

'Who else are we expecting?'

'No one.' He sat up, swung his legs down and round, and rose to his feet. 'But it's a twelve-hour flight, so the crew outnumber us by six to one.'

She paused mid-step, a flicker of alarm skittering across her face. 'Won't we be stopping for a refuel?'

'No need. The distance we're travelling is well within range.'

'I see.'

'Is that a problem?'

'Not at all,' she said, heading for the table by the window and settling herself into a seat with a quick smile that didn't quite reach her eyes.

'Are you sure?'

'Quite sure.'

'You seem a little put out by the thought.'

'I'm fine.'

Clearly she wasn't, Santi reflected as he folded himself into the seat opposite her, and watched lazily as she set her bag on the floor and extracted her laptop. But that suited him just fine, because a twitchy Thalia was a vulnerable Thalia, and with any luck that would make her even more susceptible to seduction.

'So let's get started,' she said briskly, placing the device on the table between them and opening the lid.

'With what?'

'Work.'

He arched an eyebrow. 'Now?'

'Yes.'

'We haven't even taken off yet,' he observed, making himself comfortable and loosely fastening his seatbelt. 'What's the hurry?'

'We're busy people.'

'I'm not. I have no demands at all on my time at the moment. Apart from breakfast.' And the plans he had for her.

'Well, I am, I do, and I've already had breakfast,' she said. 'And as you pointed out earlier, this is a twelve-hour flight. We might as well make use of it and knock off one day of the ten. What else are we going to do with the time?'

Santi could think of many things they could do with the time. At the rear of the plane was a cabin that had a super-king-size bed in it and a lockable door. He could keep her busy in there for hours, proving to her over and over again how much she'd once liked his swagger and his brash, uncouth ways.

Alternatively, she could continue to try and control the situation he'd put her in and he could amuse himself by indulging her. Last night, she'd attempted to dictate terms. This morning, she was having a crack at manipulating them. At no point was she going to succeed, of course, but she was welcome to carry on if she wished. The greater the battle, the sweeter her surrender. And surrender she would. Because, interestingly, she wasn't as immune to him as her no-nonsense approach would suggest. Now that she was in his direct line of sight he noted that her cheeks were stained with a faint flush. The pulse at the base of her neck was fluttering madly. She was sitting bolt upright, as if terrified of any part of her body bumping into any part of his, and she was taking great pains not to look at him.

She was nothing but a fraud, he thought with satisfaction as the engines fired up and they started to taxi to the runway. Seducing her would be the easiest thing he'd ever done. Revenge would be his in no time at all. And so he sat back, stretched out his legs beneath the table in deliberate provocation, and said with a smouldering smile, 'I'm sure we'll think of something.'

The trouble, Thalia reflected half an hour into the flight, was that despite her best intentions to ignore Santi's irritating effect on her, she could only think of one thing. And that one thing was, unfortunately, sex.

It had started the minute she'd stepped aboard and seen him reclining on the sofa, barefoot, dishevelled and louchely gorgeous. His arms had been raised, his hands behind his head. His black polo shirt had ridden up to reveal a thin band of tanned skin just above the waistband of his jeans. Her mouth had instantly dried, her pulse had spiked and then begun to thunder, and the bolt of desire that had shot through her had wiped her head of almost all rational thought. To her absolute horror, she'd wanted to throw herself on top of him and kiss him until neither of them could think straight, which had once been her wont.

As if that hadn't been unsettling enough, he'd then mentioned the size of his plane. To anyone other than him, she might have made a sly remark about anatomical over-compensation. But she knew from experience that he had absolutely nothing to worry about in that area, and God, why had she even been *thinking* about that area when it bore no relevance to anything?

Now, as they climbed to forty-five thousand feet, he was eating the breakfast that had been brought to the table by an obliging member of the cabin crew, and even that was a torturous event to witness.

'So what have you been up to since we last saw each other?' he asked while she tried to keep her eyes off his big strong hands and insanely sexy mouth as he devoured a plate of fruit and bread and downed endless cups of black coffee.

Nothing that she was going to tell him about, she thought, with a shudder of something that could have been recoil at the idea of spilling her innermost angst, but could equally have been longing. 'Work, mainly. You?'

'Same. Until six weeks ago.'

'What made you sell your business?'

'The offer I was made was too good to refuse.'

'Do you miss it?'

'No. I'd taken it as far as I could. I know when to pull out.'

She disagreed. It had always been far too soon for her liking. Panting against each other, limbs trembling and hearts thundering while they put themselves back together, she hadn't been able to tell where she stopped and he started, and if she'd had her way he'd have stayed lodged deep inside her for ever. But, dammit, these were wholly inappropriate and utterly atrocious thoughts to be having, so she ruthlessly scrubbed them from her head and vowed to keep her mind out of the gutter.

'What are you going to do next?' she said, recalling with effort what they'd been discussing and willing the heat raging through her to subside. 'Apart from your philanthropic endeavours, I mean.'

'I thought I'd invest in startups,' he said, directing a killer smile at the attendant who'd materialised to remove his now empty plate and cup. 'Mentor young entrepreneurs. Dabble with an app or two. I don't yet have a firm plan. I've had other things on my mind.'

'Such as?'

'There's a project I'm working on.' He turned the smile on her, a wicked glint sparking in the dark depths of his eyes, and for a moment she felt as dazzled as if she were staring into the sun. 'A mergers and acquisitions type of affair.'

She blinked and forced herself to focus. 'Going well?'

'It's in the early stages of development, but I have no doubt it'll be successful.'

'Good luck with it.'

'Thank you.'

See? This is the way forward. Polite small talk.

'Have you had much time for dating?'

His eyebrows rose at her question, but he could not be more surprised by it than she was—because what the hell? Since when did his dating habits constitute small talk? 'I've had no time for it at all.'

Why that came as a such a relief she really couldn't

fathom. She didn't even know why she'd asked. She wasn't remotely interested. He could date the entire world if he felt like it, and now she had to act like it was no big deal that she'd asked. 'I've had loads of time for it myself.'

'I'm sure you're leaving a trail of broken hearts wherever you go,' he said dryly, as if he could somehow tell she was lying. Which was annoying, because the last thing she wanted was him reading her mind when it was in such chaos. 'How's the family?'

Currently causing her a whole lot of grief, although she welcomed the change of subject, because discussing hearts in any shape or form with him felt unwise in the extreme. And besides, if anyone was in danger of breaking hearts, it was him. Not that their relationship had lasted long enough to get to that stage, of course.

'Very well indeed.'

'Did I read that your mother has just relieved the eleventh Duchess of Swinburne of her husband?'

'Quite possibly,' she said, wincing a little on the inside. 'I don't keep track of her antics but it does sound like something she'd do. That marriage has been on the rocks for years but that's no excuse. She's mad, bad and dangerous to know.'

'Like mother, like daughter.'

What? Was he serious? 'That's a terrible thing to say,' she said, outraged. 'I'm none of those things. I've certainly never broken up a marriage. Thanks to her behaviour, I'm not remotely scandalous.'

'It was meant to be a compliment.'

For a moment, she just stared at him. 'In what world would that be considered a compliment?'

'You have certain skills that could make a man lose his head.'

She was not going to enquire. His eyes were almost black and his smile was smouldering and she knew perfectly well what skills he was referring to, although he was the only man to ever bring them out in her. With him, she'd done things she'd never done before. She'd trusted him implicitly. Only heaven knew why. And why had he even brought it up?

'Don't be ridiculous,' she said, but she couldn't deny it did send a certain frisson through her to know that he thought of her that way. 'You didn't lose yours.'

'Didn't I?'

Of course he hadn't. She hadn't lost hers either. Their fling had lasted only three months and it had been almost entirely about sex. They'd known every inch of each other's bodies, but of each other's minds…? Not quite so much. 'Don't think I don't know what you're doing,' she said, narrowing her eyes at him.

'What's that?'

'For some inexplicable reason, you're taking great delight in trying to unsettle me. But it won't work. I'm not interested in a trip down memory lane, Santi. I'm here to work, and that's it.'

'Noted.'

Reminding herself that she did not care what he thought of her in any way other than the professional, Thalia pulled herself together and sat a little more upright. But at the same time Santi shifted in his seat, his knee bumping against hers, and if she hadn't still had her seatbelt fastened she'd have jumped a foot in the air. Every nerve-ending she possessed jolted. Her entire body flushed with heat, and she could not have been more appalled.

'My apologies,' he said, seemingly unaware of the effect the contact had had on her, thank God. 'I should have specified a larger table.'

'You could always move to another one.'

'I'm enjoying the view at this one.'

Yes, well, she wasn't. She was finding this whole experience very uncomfortable indeed. The conversation was both excruciating and baffling, and the thought of having to endure another eleven hours of it, and him, filled her with despair. 'I could do with stretching my legs.'

'Why don't I show you around?'

Show her around? Luxurious as the space was, it wasn't exactly palatial. She didn't need a tour. She just needed to get away from his penetrating gaze and re-group. But within a nanosecond of her getting up, he had too, and a moment later, he'd taken her elbow—completely unnecessarily—and propelled her down the plane to the cabin at the rear, which she hadn't realised existed until he opened the door and ushered her in.

'The bed is custom made,' he said, while she made appreciative noises and battled images of the two of them writhing around on top of it. 'The sheets have a three hundred thread count and the blankets are made from vicuna wool. The wet room can comfortably fit two and there's enough water for four twenty-minute showers. More importantly, the door is soundproofed.'

Why was he telling her this? she wondered dazedly, trying and failing to not think about all the beds and showers they'd once shared and the noise they might have made while doing so. The level of detail and the lingering felt deliberate, but was he simply proud of his new toy or was he still messing with her? She was feeling so lightheaded in the confined quarters that she couldn't begin to work it out. All she knew was that she had to vacate the room before she pushed him onto the bed and got him out of his clothes.

Thalia returned to her seat, hot and shivery and in even greater discomfort than before, and as she'd suspected the flight went downhill from then on. Santi kept looking at her when there was no need and smiling at her as if he knew something she didn't. He constantly invaded her space and filled her vision, and if he accidentally touched her one more time, a brush here, a bump there, she would not be responsible for her actions.

Over a lunch of prawns, salmon and the prettiest arrangement of tropical fruit she'd ever seen, all she'd been able to focus on were his hands and mouth, both of which she wanted on her again. In the afternoon, she tried to send some emails—a suitable replacement for her at the foundation still needed to be found, after all—and to engage in the conversation he initiated, but it was impossible to concentrate. Her imagination, sparked by the earlier tour and the distressingly appealing notion of being mad, bad and dangerous to know, had gone into overdrive. It was unhelpfully creating scenarios in which sudden turbulence tumbled them to the sofa or he simply reached for her hand and bore her off to the bed in the cabin, while she put up not one iota of resistance.

If only there was a need to refuel, she thought desperately, closing her eyes in the hope of a much-needed nap and a break from the scalding looks and the stomach-flipping smiles. She could really have done with a midway stop. It was unbelievably hot in here, there seemed to be a problem with the oxygen supply and she hated being so affected by someone who had once had—and might still have—such a low opinion of her.

But there wasn't. And there was little point regretting that she hadn't had the wherewithal last night to tell him in no uncertain terms that she'd make her own way to Brazil, so she'd have to get through what was left of the nightmare by gritting her teeth, steeling her nerves and counting down the minutes.

At least she'd get some respite on landing. She'd ordered a car to meet her at the airport and booked herself into the Bellavista, a hotel near his house, the address of which she already knew because they'd once had a conversation about where he lived and she'd later looked it up on Google Earth.

Once there, she intended to spend the evening reminding herself of why she could not and would not surrender to the attraction and giving herself a stern talking-to about resolve and inner strength. She would develop tactics to stop wondering if his hair was as soft as she remembered and his mouth as clever. She would train herself to recall the way they'd ended and how sad and hurt she'd felt in the aftermath instead.

Come tomorrow, she was sure, after a good night's sleep and some distance, her defences would be fortified, work would start and everything would be back on track.

To Santi's surprise, two cars waited on the tarmac that shimmered in the uncharacteristically sizzling heat of a mid-September afternoon. One he recognised, the other he did not. At the bottom of the steps, Thalia said, 'As it's nine p.m. Greek time, I'll head to my hotel now. See you tomorrow morning at eight,' and by the time he'd recovered from his shock enough to figure out what was going on, she'd collected her suitcase, climbed into her car and driven off.

Up until that moment he'd been congratulating himself on a flight well spent. He hadn't missed an opportunity to push his agenda and, judging by the skittishness that had intensified with every smile he'd flashed at her, he definitely had her rattled. She'd been frequently distracted. More than once he'd caught her staring at him with a darkening gaze and a hitch to her breathing when she thought he wasn't looking, and it was clear that she was halfway into his bed already.

This move of hers with the convertible and the hotel was an unanticipated development, he was perfectly willing to admit, as he donned a pair of sunglasses and watched her disappear into the dusty distance, but it didn't present a problem. There was only one hotel in the vicinity and it was in dire need of a new roof.

Striding towards the low-slung sports car the colour of anthracite, Santi pulled out his phone and made a call. Twenty minutes later and several hundreds of thousands of Brazilian reals poorer, he arrived home. Half an hour after that, as expected, so did Thalia.

'My hotel has had to close suddenly,' she announced, getting out of the car and slamming the door shut behind her, her jaw tight and her colour high. 'For two whole weeks.'

Standing in the entrance, leaning nonchalantly against the doorframe, Santi rubbed a hand over his bare chest and feigned concern. 'Oh?'

'A fire in the kitchen.'

'That is unfortunate.'

'Extremely.'

'Was anyone hurt?'

'No.'

'A relief.'

'For whom?' She stalked to the back of the vehicle and jabbed at the key to pop the boot. 'I did explain I don't need to be fed, but apparently the establishment now poses a health and safety risk. I was told the nearest open hotel is over a hundred kilometres away, which is inconvenient to say the least. I can hardly sleep in the car for the next ten days so I'm going to have to stay with you.'

Of course she was. That had never been in doubt. She was not and never would be in control of anything that was happening here. But it wouldn't hurt to

let her think she was. To lull her into a false sense of
security and then sweep the rug from under her feet.
And besides, he wanted her to come to his bed hap-
pily and willingly, not furiously and grudgingly. So
he'd let her recover tonight and up the ante tomorrow.
'I'll take your case.'
     'I can manage.'
     'Follow me.'

Well, this was just *great*, Thalia thought as she followed Santi, who'd completely ignored her point about
managing and had lifted her case out of the car as
if it was filled with air instead of ten days' worth
of belongings, into the house. First, there'd been the
shock of his dramatic reappearance in her life, and
his wholly outrageous blackmail that had upended
her weekend. Then she'd had to contend with uncontrollable, disruptive lust, which would not leave her
alone. And now, to top it all off, the fiasco of a fire
had landed her here, his house, for the next ten days.

What a twenty-four hours. The entire world seemed
to be conspiring against her. So much for respite and
a pep talk. So much for fortifying her defences and
everything being on track. She felt utterly defeated.
So exhausted that even her bones ached. She'd barely
slept a wink last night. Her earlier attempt at napping
had not been a success. As a result of the excruciat-
ingly stressful and long flight, her ankles and feet
were swollen and her skin felt like sandpaper. She
couldn't work out what time it was where, and to add
insult to injury, while she'd been desperately begging

the hotel receptionist to let her stay, Santi had apparently showered and changed into khaki shorts and a loose white shirt of which he hadn't bothered to do up even one button. He looked cool and refreshed and unfairly gorgeous; she looked a mess. And it really shouldn't matter, but somehow it did.

'Dinner will be ready in an hour,' he said, setting her suitcase down beside the bed, which stood in the centre of a large room that had white walls and polished dark wood floors.

'I'm not hungry.'

'Are you sure about that?'

She wasn't sure about anything. Least of all the knowing gleam in his eye. Something about this whole situation didn't feel quite right, but she couldn't put her finger on what was amiss. Her brain was frazzled. She was dead on her feet. Keeping her eyes and hands off his bare chest was taking up her last few drops of energy. She just wanted to clean up, take care of the throbbing ache between her legs and pass out. 'Quite sure.'

'If you need anything, my room is just across the hall.'

'Goodnight, Santi.'

'It's only half past six.'

'Not back home it isn't,' she said and shoved him out of the room.

CHAPTER FOUR

THE TROUBLE WITH crashing out early and forgetting about jetlag was that it could lead to a person spending much of the night awake. And so when Thalia's alarm went off at seven the following morning, all she wanted to do was roll over and go back to sleep. But, as she had important work to do, she levered herself out of bed, showered and dressed and then, armed with her laptop, went in search of the kitchen and a much-needed coffee.

She'd been too weary and dejected yesterday to take in any of her surroundings. But now, despite still feeling gritty-eyed and groggy today, she was able to observe that beyond the first-floor bedroom wing, much of the house didn't appear to have any walls. Mostly it seemed to be built around trees, multi-levelled platforms on stilts, thick gnarled branches pushing through the thatched roof. Here, there was a vast decked open-air living space with views over the sparkling sea. There, a wide staircase swept round and down to verdant gardens and the golden beach beyond. She'd been to some spectacular properties over the years—her ultra-wealthy family owned a number of them across the globe, in fact—but she'd never seen anything quite like this. Rustic and sprawling, it seemed to emerge from the lush vegetation as if having grown from seed. Every inch revealed some new architectural or natural curiosity.

The clink of crockery and the heavenly scent of brewed coffee led her down the stairs and, unexpectedly, outside. Bracing herself for a renewed assault on her fragile senses from her host, on the defences she hadn't yet found the energy to strengthen, Thalia took a deep breath and pulled her shoulders back.

But she was still unprepared for the sharp punch to the chest she experienced when she saw Santi lounging at a table beneath a huge parasol by the pool, facing in her direction. He was wearing nothing but a pair of black board shorts and mirrored sunglasses. His tan was deep and his muscles were as defined as she remembered. He looked like a model, posing solely for her entertainment, and God, how on earth was she supposed to concentrate with all this physical perfection on display?

Swallowing hard and reminding herself that in ten minutes, at precisely eight a.m., work would begin— because she would *not* be thwarted again—Thalia willed her racing pulse to slow, dug deep for composure and forced herself to move forwards.

'You have a very interesting home,' she said, inanely grasping onto the only thought in her head that wasn't revolving around the appallingly inappropriate urge to straddle his lap, plant her hands on his chest and crush her mouth to his.

'I like it.'

'Have you lived here for long?'

'Eight years. I bought the land and built the house with the first million I made.'

'Its design must be pretty unique.'

'It affords me privacy and space and I appreciate nature.'

She appreciated nature too. Especially when it looked like him. Maybe keeping her eyes on the distant hills across the water instead of the ridges and bumps of his abs would help with her concentration.

'Come and take a seat,' he said, indicating the chair next to him, the only chair in sight.

'Thanks.' Thalia pulled it out, dragged it as far from his as possible without being obvious and sat down, facing the sea.

'Coffee?'

'Yes, please.'

'Help yourself to breakfast.'

'It all looks delicious,' she said, piling a plate with guava, papaya and pastries to make up for her missed supper the evening before, while he filled a cup and pushed it in her direction.

'Did you sleep well?'

No. 'Yes, thank you.'

'I trust you were comfortable in your room.'

She should have been because it was airy, cool, simply furnished and in theory very restful. She could touch the trees from the generous balcony. The voile curtains that fluttered at the wide-open doors added to the whimsical serenity. Before falling into bed last night she'd spent a good hour in the ensuite bathroom with its huge, high-pressure rain showerhead that made her think of the Iguazu Falls, not that she'd ever been. The only problem with the room was its location, across the hall from his—so he'd said—and not in a hotel five kilometres away. 'It's charming.'

'Mine is similar but double the size.'

'How lovely,' she replied, determinedly not envisaging his gorgeous, bronzed body tangled up in snowy white sheets, but instead drinking deeply of the coffee he had made— just the way she liked it—and taking strength from the hit of super-strong caffeine.

Their sleeping arrangements were irrelevant, she told herself firmly. The *only* thing that mattered for the next ten days was making a success of this situation. Proving to herself that she had talent and ability in the field she loved and that she was able to survive perfectly well on her own. She'd get used to the way he made her feel. Over time it might even diminish so as to be undetectable. It was simply a question of mind over matter. Finding her inner strength and focusing on the long-term goal, which was not going to be obstructed by anything or anyone.

'So I've identified a good spot for a workstation,' she said, setting down her cup and stabbing a fork into a piece of papaya. 'Upstairs on the deck. A big table, plenty of space. It's ideal.'

'I see no reason to move.'

Her eyebrows shot up and she stared at him for a moment, fork hovering in mid-air. 'Are you suggesting we stay here by the pool?'

'Is that a problem?'

Yes, it was. She wasn't on holiday. 'Well, it's not very professional, is it?'

'I can work in a variety of locations.'

'I prefer to stick to an office.'

'It seems a shame to waste the weather.'

She glanced up at the cloudless blue sky from which beat down the morning sun, already hot and intense, and frowned. 'Isn't the weather always like this at this time of year? I thought this was the dry season.'

'Sometimes it rains.'

'All the more reason for proper shelter.'

'My house, my rules, Thalia,' he said, pausing in his slathering of butter over a slice of bread to lift his sunglasses. He ran his hot dark gaze over her smart white shirt, taupe trouser combo. 'You might want to reconsider your outfit.'

'Ditto.'

'I anticipate needing to cool off.'

That announcement was accompanied by an un-necessarily wolfish smile, and she thought that if any-one was going to need to cool off it was her. Despite the early hour she could feel a bead of sweat trick-ling between her breasts. Her skin was prickling and her blood was boiling. And all because of a scorcher of a look. 'Can't you at least put a T-shirt on in the meantime?'

'Do I bother you?'

He did. Very much. Was it his intention to wander around semi-naked the entire time she was here? How was she supposed to handle that? Had he no sense of decency? Professionalism? And how would he feel if she wafted about in nothing more than a bikini? Perhaps she should try it and see.

'Not at all,' she lied smoothly. 'I'm merely thinking of sunburn.'

'Are you offering to rub sunscreen into me?'

Thalia ignored the strong temptation to say yes and stifled a sigh. What on earth was he was he playing at? First the plane, now this. Was he flirting with her? Why? And, more importantly, how could she get him to stop?

'Why don't you tell me more about your philanthropic plans?' she said, despairing of him, herself and this whole massively inconvenient situation as she picked up a knife and sharply sliced a tiny custard tart in two. 'What sort of thing do you have in mind?'

'I'll take that as a no to the sunscreen.'

'It's eight on the dot and I won't tolerate another delay.'

Santi shifted in his seat, sending a wave of deliciously masculine scent in her direction, which she ruthlessly repelled.

'I'd like to focus on Brazil,' he said, angling his body and stretching out his long, muscled legs, which didn't help her composure at all when she could remember as if it were yesterday how they'd felt rubbing up and down against hers in various beds across the globe. 'Specifically, the underprivileged and the disadvantaged, of which there are many. I want to improve literacy. To show young kids in the favelas and elsewhere that there are ways out, and to create the opportunities to enable that.'

'These are causes that are personal to you,' she said with an understanding nod, finally in her comfort zone, thank God.

His eyebrows rose. 'How do you know that?'

'I Googled you.'

It had been one of the first things she'd done after he'd left her room the morning after her brother's wedding. She'd wanted to know everything about the man who'd repeatedly rocked her world. And she hadn't been disappointed, because information on him abounded.

He'd grown up in Rio's most dangerous favela, she'd discovered. At the time, it had been headquarters of one of the largest gangs in the city. There'd been frequent clashes among the police, local drug cartels and rival gangs. Violence and gun battles had been a regular occurrence. His schooling had been chaotic and, along with the majority of his friends, he'd dropped out for good at thirteen. With no qualifications, and therefore limited job options, most of his peers had turned to drug dealers for work, and a life of crime. He'd been one of the lucky ones, finding salvation in a library that had been running a course in coding.

She'd read for hours about how his tough, precarious upbringing had driven him to succeed, and had pored over articles detailing the stellar growth of his tech business. He'd overcome such hurdles with such enviable strength and determination it was no wonder she'd been smitten from the off.

'Background knowledge on a project is always useful,' she said sagely, as if she'd done her research for professional purposes this morning instead of over the course of many weeks, long ago, for personal ones.

'I agree.'

'Did you Google me?'

'I did,' he said with a nod. 'It took quite a while to wade through all the photos of you at various society events, but eventually I found what I was looking for.'

'And what was that?'

'Your suitability for my requirements.'

Oh.

'One article I read said you became interested in the idea of charity after watching a programme on global poverty as a kid and being deeply affected by it. You rounded up unwanted toys and clothes at home and found ways of putting them to good use. At school you ran an annual designer clothing sale and raised thousands for good causes. You have a masters in charity management and went straight from university to work at the family foundation where you've been ever since.'

Every word of what he said was true, she thought, reminding herself sternly that she didn't *want* him to be interested in her personally. She even recalled the interview—one of the few she'd ever given, since the foundation had a PR department for that sort of thing.

What she hadn't revealed at the time or at any moment since, however, was where those unwanted toys and clothes had come from. They certainly hadn't come from her parents, as might have naturally been expected. Before he'd died from a heart attack when she was a teenager, her stern, aristocratic father had only had time for her eldest brother, Leo, who'd been destined to take over the family empire since birth. Her mother had always been too busy jetting around the world and causing scandals to acknowledge any of her children's existence unless it suited her. It was the nannies who'd overcompensated for this criminal lack of parental attention by showering her and her siblings with material possessions, as if those could *ever* make up for bewilderingly wilful neglect.

She'd only emerged relatively unscathed because she'd had Atticus to cling to. While the others had floundered, each in their own way, she'd turned to him to celebrate her successes and lament her failures. He was the one who'd talked her through friendship dramas and teenage angst when there'd been no one else. He'd been her rock, and she'd always believed that she'd been his.

But she didn't want to think about her twin right now, about everything she'd had and all she'd now lost. She wasn't even sure any more what that was. Lately she'd been wondering if perhaps their bond hadn't been as strong for him as it had for her, if the need for support and security had been hers alone. She'd had a smattering of boyfriends, but she'd never managed to find the same depth of connection with any of them. Yet Atticus had met and married Zoe with no trouble at all. He hadn't thought twice about sacrificing their closeness and casting her aside. Could he have found her a nuisance all these years? Could he too have been indulging her while sighing on the inside? The possibility of that being the case was too much to bear.

'I've had every privilege going,' she said, swallowing down the sudden lump in her throat and yanking herself out of the painful past and back to the present, 'and I've always felt that that comes with enormous responsibility. But more than that, it was simply always what I've wanted to do.'

'Your resume is impressive.'

'That's what you paid for. And speaking of which, have you had any thoughts about fundraising?'

He shook his head. 'Not yet.'

'Any idea who you'd like on the board?'

'None.'

'Do you even have a name for your venture?'

'No.'

'We *are* going to be busy.'

Thalia clearly wanted to get underway, in order to be done as quickly as possible, but Santi felt no such urge. He was quite content to draw things out for as long as it pleased him, and screwing with her attempts to engage him in the details of his project would satisfy his need for control. So every time she tried to drill down into the minutiae of what he wanted to achieve, or brainstorm mission statements, he found he had a phone call to make or a swim to take. A drink to fetch or food to prepare. These pronouncements were met by frowns and sighs and much gritting of the teeth, but he was not remotely deterred, even though by mid-afternoon the frustration was rolling off her in waves and he could practically see the steam coming from her ears.

'You look hot,' he observed from the far end of the pool, because riling her was fun and somehow it appeased his sense of injustice. 'Come and join me. The water's great.'

Evidently that was one provocation too far, because in response to his invitation Thalia slammed down the lid of her laptop and jumped to her feet.

'You're not taking this remotely seriously, are you?' she said, marching towards him, arms folded across her chest, which did interesting things to her cleavage. 'You're ruining everything we're trying to achieve. You have the attention span of a gnat. You're driving me mad. How you managed to build a billion-dollar business I have no clue.'

Grit and determination and a great idea was how he'd done it. A talent for coding, a driving need to get out of the slums after one of his friends had been shot in the chest, and sixteen-hour days spent hustling for deals. But he was not going to go into that with her. And anyway, that information, unlike some, was already in the public domain. 'What's the hurry?'

'In ten days' time I'll be gone and we won't have nailed down a thing. Your philanthropic endeavours will be dead in the water and your money completely wasted. That's the hurry.'

'You're making the mistake of assuming the days are to run consecutively.'

She stared at him, speechless for a moment, wide-eyed and open-mouthed, as if shock had rooted her to the spot. 'What?'

'You really should have been more specific with the details of your lot.'

Her brows snapped together, her jaw clenched and a flush hit her cheeks. 'I never anticipated blackmail.'

'I always get what I want.'

'Are you implying that I'll be here for as long as it suits you?'

'In a nutshell.'

She thought about that for a moment—he could almost see her brain overheating with the effort—and then she began to radiate such ire and frustration she blazed.

'This may be some sort of bizarre power trip of a game to you, but it isn't to me,' she said, her hands now on her hips as she glared down at him in glorious passionate fury, any semblance of cool long gone. 'I didn't just decide to offer up my services at the auction on a whim. My entire future career is at stake here.'

That piqued his interest. 'What do you mean?'

'I'm about to step down from the foundation,' she said hotly. 'I'm setting up a consultancy service, to help others to help others. You're my first client. You're supposed to be my success story.'

Ah. 'So that's why you turned your nose up at the thought of me hiring someone else at the gala the other night.'

'Yes,' she said through clenched teeth.

'I could make or break you.'

'In theory.'

'Interesting.'

'The only interesting thing about anything is why you're intent on sabotaging my efforts.'

Well, he wasn't telling her *that*. 'You need to keep me sweet.'

'This is impossible,' she said, throwing her hands up in utter exasperation. '*You're* impossible. We're making no progress whatsoever and you don't even seem to want to, despite claiming to be desperate for my advice and paying handsomely for it. There's absolutely no point in me being here. I'd be better off cutting my losses and starting again. Anyone who's ever tried to work with you would understand, I'm sure.'

There was every point in her being here, she was not starting again and he'd been going about seducing her in entirely the wrong way, he was beginning to realise. No wonder she was resisting the obvious chemistry. Focusing on establishing her new business clearly trumped it. So much so that he would have admired her strength of character had it not been in direct competition with his objectives.

He had to amend his tactics and appeal to her brain as well as her body. He had to show that he respected what she was trying to achieve and flatter her talents, while also continuing to fuel the attraction. His goals hadn't changed. And he *did* want her advice. For years he'd relied on the charity of others, and he'd made himself a promise long ago that as soon as he was in a position to pay that back, he would. That was why, despite allowing her to think otherwise on Sat-

57

urday night, he would never have withdrawn his fifty-million-euro donation to her foundation.

'All right,' he said, adjusting his strategy to incorporate all these new revelations and heaving himself out of the pool. 'I can see this is important to you. And it is to me, too. So let's get to work.'

CHAPTER FIVE

Now THAT SANTI had decided to cooperate—and what a blessed relief that was—they made excellent progress. He finally came up with a name and a mission statement. Thalia enlightened him about jurisdictions and structures, lawyers and accountants and PR, and then tasked him over the next few days with researching literacy programmes, building a potential board of trustees and outlining a launch event.

His brain worked dizzyingly fast, he was focused and engaged, and unlike earlier she could totally see how he'd achieved everything he had. She admired his ambition for his charity. A cause obviously close to his heart, he was taking it very seriously indeed, which made his earlier behaviour all the more incomprehensible.

'So are you going to tell me what on earth this morning was about?' she asked when they finally wrapped up at six.

Stretching the kinks out of his muscles, Santi looked at her, a picture of innocence that she didn't believe for a moment. 'What do you mean?'

'The phone calls and the swims and the constant

LUCY KING 59

provision of snacks,' she said, reflecting that all of those distractions had been a trial, although the swims had been particularly wearing.

Every time he'd dived into the pool she'd had to stop what she was doing and watch. The power with which he completed length after length had reminded her of the strength with which he'd once held her, and she'd almost fainted with longing. Their hotel-room affair had been conducted mainly indoors, occasionally on a balcony, and she feared the sight of him climbing out of the pool, with the water sluicing off his magnificent body, glistening in the sunlight, would be permanently etched into her retinas. None of it had made for an easy day. 'Does it give you a thrill to toy with me?'

'That would depend on the type of toying you're talking about,' he said with an unhelpful glint in his eye.

Well, she certainly wasn't talking about the type of toying that involved tying her to a four-poster bed in New York, working her into frenzy and then leaving her there throbbing and panting and cursing him for an hour, even if the eventual multiple orgasms had been worth it. 'How about ten days that could turn out to be twenty, thirty or whatever you decide?' she said, gritting her teeth against the unwelcome onslaught of memories and focusing.

'There's no need to be quite so dramatic. I'm merely factoring in the weekend and the odd half-day break.'

'I don't like being manipulated.'

'Who does? But perhaps you'd like to join me for supper.'

She wouldn't particularly. She'd spent much of the day on edge and she could do with some time out of his disturbing orbit. But she'd refused the snacks on principle, hard work always gave her an appetite and her culinary skills were virtually non-existent, so pettily cutting off her nose to spite her face held little appeal.

'That would be nice,' she said grudgingly and packed up her things.

On the upstairs terrace, which had large squishy chairs and a fabulous panoramic view of the sparkling sea and the forest-covered hills of the islands beyond, Santi furnished Thalia with a glass of deliciously cold white wine and then lit the grill—a machine that came with levers and wheels like something out of the Industrial Revolution.

Within moments, the scent of woodsmoke filled the warm evening air, and it made her think of the hotel she should have been staying at, where there'd been no such smell, which was odd because surely a fire significant enough to close down the entire establishment would have left some trace. There hadn't even been any visible smoke, now she thought about it. Had it been windy? She couldn't remember.

'You really love what you do, don't you?'

Setting that particular conundrum to one side, Thalia switched her attention to the man sprinkling salt over churrasco like a pro with one hand and tossing a green salad with the other. 'I do,' she said, taking a moment to admire yet another of his talents.

'You're very good at it.'

'Thank you.'

'Very passionate.'

Ah. She should have known that allowing her frustration to boil over and telling him why she needed this project would come back to haunt her. 'Yes, well, I'm as determined to get what I want as you are and, as I said, there's a lot at stake for me.'

'So why leave the foundation to set up on your own?'

'It's a long and complicated story.'

'The night is young.'

'I wouldn't even know here to start.'

'Try the beginning.'

No, thanks.

'Why are you so interested?'

'We have to talk about something.'

'There are plenty of other topics of conversation.' Such as running a successful business. This country of his, which she'd never visited before despite having a girlfriend who lived in Rio. Destruction of the rain forest. That was a good one. 'I hear there are whales to be found around these parts at this time of year. That could be a fascinating discussion. I like whales.'

'We never bothered much with small talk.'

That was true, she supposed. Even their attempts on the plane had failed one way or another. But did they have to chat about *her*? She wasn't even sure she wanted to discuss the last couple of years. She never had before. She wouldn't have had anyone to share her woes with even if she did. Her mother had little time for anyone other than herself. Atticus was at the centre of her existential crisis, so he wasn't an option, and her other siblings, with whom she was trying to establish new relationships after stupidly believing for thirty years that because they didn't get her like her twin did she didn't really need them, were busy with their own lives.

Leo was wrapped up in his wife, Willow, and baby daughter, and building boats on Santorini. Zander was running the family empire from London and working his way through the world's female population. Daphne, who'd once had cancer and therefore chemotherapy, was undergoing stressful and emotional fertility treatment, and who knew where wild child Olympia was or what she was doing?

Thalia was on her own on this journey of self-discovery of hers, but that was fine. That was the whole point, and it wasn't as if she needed advice or support. She knew what she was doing, even if it did feel like a struggle sometimes. Besides, some sixth sense was warning her that it might be unwise to open up to Santi. She'd seen how ruthless he could be when he wanted something. Any hint of emotion or vulnerability and he might well weaponize it. In fact, it wouldn't surprise her in the slightest if, at some point, he used her earlier admission that she was relying on him for her future success as leverage to strong-arm her into doing what he wanted.

'We could talk about you instead,' she said with a pointed lift of her eyebrows.

'You first.'

Well, that wasn't an outright no, which was encouraging, because she found she was beginning to have questions that hadn't been answered by any article she'd ever read. About his mother, his father and how he'd handled not having one. Whether he had any advice about launching a business and what this mergers and acquisitions project he was working on entailed. Nothing too intimate, of course. She had no interest in knowing *why* he hadn't dated anyone over the last thirteen months.

Still, a quid pro quo could be the way forward. Perhaps the relentless desire she felt for him and her inability to control it were down to the fact she'd never had closure. Their breakup had been unexpectedly brutal and she'd carried the wounds of it for months. Quite possibly she still did. Maybe clearing the air— explaining where she'd been at the time and, in return, finding out why he'd thought her arrogant and shallow, and whether he continued to do so—would somehow rid her of her infatuation with him. She could only hope.

'All right,' she said, taking a fortifying mouthful of wine and bracing herself. Even though she owned her behaviour and feelings now, she wasn't proud of them, and discussing it wasn't going to be pleasant. 'You don't have siblings, do you?'

Raking the embers with a poker, Santi didn't answer immediately. But after a moment he gave his head a faint shake and said, 'No.'

'Well, as you know, I have a twin. And having a twin—even a non-identical one—isn't like having a regular sibling. The bond is unique. It's like having a built-in best friend. Or at least that was how it was between Atticus and me. For years we knew what the other was thinking without having to say a word. We were consistently there for each other, whatever the circumstances. It was always us against the world.'

'That sounds intense.'

'It was,' she agreed with a nod. 'Very. We weren't together all the time obviously. Eventually I went to university in the UK, and he studied law in the States, and then we embarked on our respective careers. But we spoke every week. He was my go-to person for almost everything. Our connection always seemed unbreakable.'

Santi put down the poker, topped up her glass and then sank into the chair next to hers. 'Seemed?'

'When he met Zoe, everything changed,' she confessed, stifling a sigh. 'She's lovely and she makes him insanely happy, but for me it's been a difficult adjustment. I had him all to myself for thirty years. Of course he'd had girlfriends in the past but never anything serious. Then she came along and it was as if—' She shrugged. 'I don't know—she somehow stepped in and took my place. It felt like betrayal. Rejection. Loss. And it was horrible. Deep down, I hoped the relationship wouldn't last, which is awful.'

'Did you speak to him about it?'

'I considered it briefly, but what could I have said? That I was jealous? How pathetic would that have sounded?' She shook her head. 'No. I didn't want to ruin things for him. He was really happy. So I kind of avoided them, which I guess was pretty cowardly but I was so confused and upset I didn't know what else to do. When they got engaged, I couldn't kid myself any more that it was just a fling. I realised I had to figure out how to exist without him being my constant support and always at the end of the phone, and that made me assess everything else. Family. My identity. Work. I've had it so easy in my career. I didn't even question my appointment as CEO of the foundation. But then I found myself wondering why I ended up in that position and what I'm genuinely capable of. That's why I need to branch out and set up my own business. To see if I can make a success of things independently. I know it's not a real test since I'm not going to be destitute if it fails but it's the best shot I've got.'

'You won't fail.'

'I hope not.'

'The auctioneer on Saturday night was right,' said Santi. 'You *do* know what you're talking about. You *are* the ultimate expert and, from my point of view at least, there *is* nothing you don't know.'

'Yes, well, we'll see,' she said, doing her best to ignore the pride that shimmied through her at his praise and recall the purpose of this conversation. 'But in the meantime I can't allow any distractions.'

'Am I a distraction?'

He was the ultimate distraction, but he already held

way too much power in this situation, so she was not going to admit how much he still affected her. 'When we met,' she said, not quite answering the question instead, 'you were just what I needed.'

'And what was that?'

'An analeptic.'

'In what way?'

'Even though I was so pleased for them, I found Atticus and Zoe's wedding incredibly tough, and I know that makes me a not very nice person, but that's how it was. It was as if his life was suddenly going off in a completely different direction and I was being left behind, alone and adrift. I was miserable that evening and just wanted something else to think about.'

'Me.'

She nodded. 'You.'

'I had no idea you were feeling that way,' he said with a frown that suggested he was faintly offended by the knowledge.

'I hope no one did. I tried hard to hide it. But you made all those ugly shameful emotions disappear,' she said, remembering with the ghost of a smile how completely bowled over she'd been by him. 'You made *everything* disappear. I'd never experienced attraction like it. You were supposed to be a one-night stand but the sex was so mind-blowing I couldn't help but want more and so it became an affair. You were a wonderful escape from reality. When I was with you I didn't have to think about anything else. And when I wasn't with you I didn't have to think about anything else either, because you and what we were doing together were in my head pretty much all the time. Normally my relationships fizzle out pretty quickly—not that there've been that many of them—but ours didn't and the longer it went on the more I began to realise that it had to stop. I'd switched one dependency for another. How could I work out who I was on my own if I wasn't ever *on* my own? I needed space and time to work on myself. I still do. I had planned to tell you all this. That morning in Paris I was going to explain everything. But before I could, you said all those horrible things and I went into shock and after that I didn't think you deserved the truth.'

Finally at the end of her confession, Thalia stopped and drained the last of her wine, her heart pounding and her mouth dry. But actually, voicing that truth hadn't been so bad. Perhaps she'd spent so long analysing what she'd thought and how she'd felt, she'd become inured to it. Santi looked a bit shellshocked, though, which was understandable because it was a lot to take in. But at least she'd got it off her chest. At least she'd told him about Paris and clarified in no uncertain terms why she could not give in to the chemistry again. Now she could switch the focus to him and drill down into how he'd ever got the idea that she thought she was better than him.

'I see,' he said, although he probably didn't see at all because he didn't have siblings, let alone a twin, so how could he?

'I told you it was complicated.'

'You were right.'

* * *

Muttering something about the grill being ready for the meat, Santi got to his feet and thought that 'complicated' had to be the understatement of the century. Never in a million years would he have guessed that Thalia had had all that going on. At no point in any of the conversations they'd had while in the throes of their affair had she said anything about her relationship with Atticus or how she felt about it. But then they hadn't really talked about much apart from logistics. There'd been little inclination to chat when they'd met up in person. Mostly they'd communicated with their bodies.

He picked up a pair of tongs and transferred the churrasco to the grill, and as it began to sizzle he wondered what to make of her many astonishing revelations, some of which could have the potential to blow the assumptions he'd been living with for months to smithereens.

Did they have any implications for his pursuit of vengeance?

Had they put a different spin on things?

No. Nothing had changed. Her explanation for why she'd ended their relationship made a certain sort of sense, and bravely holding her hands up to everything she'd thought and felt at the time was admirable, but he could never forget the chilly disdain and sheer disgust with which she'd looked at him in that Parisian hotel room, and the need to get the upper hand with her and restore control still burned deep within him.

Sentimentality had no place in this scheme of his,

he reminded himself grimly, and he had no intention of quitting it, so he wouldn't think about how tough the last couple of years must have been for her. He wouldn't envisage her miserable and confused and made increasingly wretched by her brother's happiness. That her mind had been equally blown by the sex they'd had together was of no interest to him at all. How into him she'd been was as irrelevant as how into her he'd been. None of it mattered. Not her previous relationships, not her insecurities and how she was overcoming them, not the oddly jarring discovery that she'd been using him.

Above all, he would not dwell on the fact that he'd lied about having siblings because that can of worms did not need opening. In any case, these days he hardly ever thought of the father who'd disowned him before he was born or the socialite supermodel half-sister he'd never met. The one time, years ago, when he'd dared to venture into the exclusive neighbourhood in which he'd discovered they lived—so very different from the shack in the favela he called home—barely crossed his mind any more.

He would tell Thalia anything she wanted to know about his life now—and he had no doubt that she would be imminently holding him to account and pressing him for details—but that particular part of his past, with the dangerous anger and resentment it had provoked and the unsettling intrusion it could make into the present if he let it, would never be up for discussion.

'So what was your upbringing like?' she asked predictably the minute he put the sliced churrasco on the table she'd moved to and sat down.

'The diametric opposite of yours, I imagine.'

Her eyebrows rose, her expression cool. 'You know nothing about mine.'

'I can guess.' Opportunity, security, everything money could buy...

'I very much doubt it.'

He handed her the tongs. 'Then enlighten me.'

'My father was stern and authoritarian and believed that children should be seen and not heard,' she said as she helped herself to some meat. 'My mother embarked on a string of affairs virtually the minute the ink was dry on the marriage certificate. She was— and is—so busy gallivanting across the world she was rarely around. Parental affection and support were non-existent. We were all basically brought up by nannies. Materially, we wanted for nothing but the money just meant that the neglect and dysfunction were easier to hide.'

Santi reeled. She was right. He couldn't have guessed. 'None of that appeared in any of the articles I read,' he said, having to reassess his assumptions once again, which was not a particularly comfortable experience, since he was rarely wrong and didn't much like it.

'I know.' She put down the tongs and added some salad to her plate. 'Selene's affairs and scandalous behaviour are well-documented but the rest of it is our little secret. I don't know how I'd have coped with it all without Atticus. Who do you have to face the challenges of life with?'

He had no one, and that was fine with him. Allowing people to get close raised the possibility of rejection, and all the wild emotions that came with it, and who needed that? 'Friends,' he said, although the people he hung out with were really more acquaintances.

'How did you feel about not having a father?'

'It was nothing unique,' he said easily as he served himself, giving her the answer he'd given to so many so often before. 'You can't miss what you don't have.'

'I would say that's a shame but sometimes fathers aren't all they're cracked up to be.'

It was on the tip of his tongue to agree but he bit back the words. Just because she too had suffered rejection at the hands of hers did not mean that his experience had to be shared. It wasn't as if he was after understanding or catharsis. He'd come to terms with his past years ago, so he had no need to talk about anything. The mere thought of where such a conversation might lead—exposure, vulnerability, weakness—turned his stomach and chilled his blood.

'Although I do feel that family is important, however rubbish,' she added. 'I wouldn't be without any of mine.'

'I wouldn't know.'

'What was your mother like?'

Desperate. Helpless. Fragile. Everything he'd determined not to be. 'She died fifteen years ago.' Three years before he'd had the money to pluck her out of the favela, which was something he'd always regret.

'That wasn't what I asked.'

'She was typical of her environment.'

'Which was?'

Wretched. Filled with such danger and threat that he did his best not to think about it, let alone talk about it. 'You must have read up on it,' he said in an effort to deflect her as he spooned some chimichurri onto his plate.

'I'm after the story behind the headlines.'

A faint shudder ran through him. 'There is no story.'

'There must be.'

Well, she wasn't getting it. 'Let's eat.'

Thalia was not remotely surprised when Santi called it a night shortly after they'd cleared their plates. She'd spilled her guts and she'd felt it only fair that he did the same. He, however, had evidently thought otherwise. He'd shut down all further attempts to converse along the lines of anything except business, and even that topic had run dry after a while. If she hadn't been so annoyed by it she'd have been impressed by his skill at avoiding answering her more personal questions with anything other than lines that sounded as though he'd delivered them a thousand times before.

But she wasn't convinced you couldn't miss what you didn't have and she didn't buy his story about there not being a story behind the story. Despite the outwardly relaxed pose, a tiny muscle had visibly throbbed in his cheek and his smile had tightened, which suggested that he definitely had something to hide. Would she ever find out what that was? Who knew?

There was one thing, however, she did know. The quid pro quo she'd tried to make happen had not materialised, and therefore she was not telling him anything else. She was through with talking. She'd revealed too much already without getting anything in return, and enough was enough. On more than one front, come to think of it, because she was fed up with being constantly on the back foot and having to scrabble about for control.

So that was it for conversation and compliance. Santi could count the days whichever way he chose. She was counting them consecutively, and if she decided to start at seven and end at eight so she could finish earlier there was nothing he could do to stop her. They were her hours as much as his, so from here on in she'd be making no further attempt to clear up the past. She'd find some other way to draw a line under them and move on. In the meantime, all she'd be focusing on was work.

CHAPTER SIX

ONE UNINTENDED CONSEQUENCE of shutting down the conversation when it cut a little too close to the bone, Santi came to realise the following morning, was a cool and clipped Thalia who could barely bring herself to look at him, which was immensely irritating since it presented a major setback in his plans to seduce her.

Unfortunately, this state of affairs did not improve with the passage of time. He upped the wattage of his smiles but they failed to pierce her frostiness. Every attempt he made to engage her in conversation fell on stony ground, and by lunchtime he'd decided that the situation could not be allowed to continue. He *would* get her into his bed, she *would* end up falling for him and he *would* then leave her high and dry. And so, as he had no intention of opening up to her as she'd tried so hard to get him to do at supper, he figured he was just going to have to thaw her another way.

'We're taking the afternoon off,' he announced, once lunch had been cleared from the poolside table by the housekeeper, who came in three times a week to restore order to the place and restock his fridge.

'I'm not,' Thalia countered with a chilly smile as she returned her attention to her laptop.

'I feel we could do with a break. The last forty-eight hours have been pretty intense. And it is very hot.'

'You can do whatever you wish but I'm expecting an important call.'

She'd have to mount a far better objection than that to deter him. 'Phones are mobile these days,' he said dryly.

'Very amusing,' she said, clearly not in the slightest bit amused.

'I've had reports that a pod of whales has been sighted nearby. I thought we could take a look.'

A flicker of interest skittered across her face— there and gone in a flash, but evidence enough that he'd found a weak spot to exploit. 'You go and fill me in when you get back.'

'There'd be no need to make up the hours, if that's what's concerning you.'

'That's not concerning me at all.'

'The boat has Wi-Fi.'

'I'd expect nothing less.'

'Perfect for phone calls.'

'And yet I find I'm still able to resist.'

Not for much longer. 'The whales are travelling with calves.'

As he'd anticipated, that did give her pause for thought. She went still, a faint frown creasing her brow, her beautiful brown eyes narrowing minutely. 'Calves?'

'Lots of them,' he said, sensing victory and closing

in on it. 'It's a rare thing to see. A once-in-a-lifetime experience, I'm told.'

'How far away are they?'

'About four miles off the coast.'

Her frown deepened, as if she were waging some internal battle, and then she said, 'So we could be there and back in, say, a couple of hours?'

Well, in theory, they could, he thought with a mental air punch of triumph. But in practice they weren't returning until she'd lost the attitude and the seduction was back on track. 'Perhaps even less if we get going now.'

'I'll fetch my things.'

Having made some calculations with regards to distance, time and speed—for both the boat and the whales—Santi took the scenic route and he took it slow. He motored them between uninhabited islands, into the sparkling turquoise shallows of forested coves fringed with golden sands and around jagged rocks that jutted into the sea, before heading out into open water and speeding across the ocean to their ultimate destination.

Initially, and quite probably deliberately, Thalia positioned herself at the bow of the boat, as far from him as it was possible to get. But, as he'd anticipated, the heat of the afternoon sun and the spectacular scenery eventually melted her enough to join him on the flybridge, where he warmed her up further with idle and non-threatening conversation—which was how he came to learn that she loved swimming and loathed coriander.

On arrival at the recommended spot some fifty minutes after they'd departed, he switched off the motor yacht's engine. As they bobbed about on the sea in the vicinity of the few other boats that had heard the news and gathered there, he opened the hamper of drinks and snacks his housekeeper had prepared, then handed her a bottle of chilled sparkling water and extracted one for himself.

'So this is a pleasant way to spend a Tuesday afternoon, don't you think?' he said, sitting down beside her and stretching out his legs.

'I'd rather be getting on with our project,' she replied dryly. But she was smiling faintly as she cracked open the lid, and she didn't edge away, which was encouraging. 'However, it is rather lovely to be on the water. I've always found it very relaxing. I can't remember the last time I was out on a boat. Ironic really when half the family fortune comes from shipping, but I've been so busy lately there hasn't been much time for relaxation.'

'I know what you mean.'

She took a long sip of water, which was more arresting an action than he'd ever considered before, and then set the bottle on the table. 'How long have you had it?'

He cleared his throat and scrubbed his head of the urge to set his lips to her neck, which would no doubt earn him a shove into the table. 'Seven years,' he said, just about managing to recall her question. 'I acquired it as soon as I had a jetty to moor it to.'

'It doesn't look as though it's simply for show.'

It wasn't, which was why it could probably do with a repaint. 'Why would I have a boat simply for show?'

'It can happen when one has billions in the bank.'

'You'd know about that better than me.'

'I've never really seen the point of trophies.'

'Neither have I, despite having been bombarded with offers the second the sale of my company hit the press. The plane is purely practical.'

'Where do you go?'

'In this?' She nodded. 'Up and down the coast. The furthest I've been so far is Natal, just over a thousand nautical miles north of here. It's the easternmost point of the country. Do you know it?'

She shook her head, the sun glinting off her shades. 'This is the first time I've been to Brazil. I have a friend in Rio, who I've been meaning to visit for ages, but somehow I've never got round to it. That now seems a shame. I messaged her to see if she'd like to meet up when I'm done here but I haven't heard back yet.'

The offer to take her into the city and show her around was on the tip of his tongue, an urge insisting it be voiced, but with a flicker of alarm Santi bit it back. He tended to avoid Rio if he could, since it held few good memories, and acting as a tour guide wasn't what these ten days were about. He didn't know why he'd even thought of it when, this trip aside, he had no intention of taking her anywhere other than his bed.

'It's a vast country to explore,' he said, rubbing away the bead of sweat that he could suddenly feel at his temple.

'What made you choose to live on the coast?'

'I like being able to look out into nothing but blue sky, space and endless possibilities.'

'Quite the contrast to the favela, I imagine.'

His eyebrows lifted. 'How very perceptive of you.'

'I can be.'

Not if he had any say in the matter. He didn't want her poking around in his psyche. Even he tried not to go there if he could help it. And he was supposed to be quizzing and mellowing her, not the other way round. 'Where does your interest in whales come from?' he asked, vaguely wondering where the hell the sea breeze was.

'When I was ten, I saw a documentary on them and was hooked,' she said. 'They're an extremely so-cial and caring species. They protect each other and nurture their young. I found that novel yet appealing, even back then. I still do.'

'With your upbringing, I'm not surprised.'

'I see I'm not the only perceptive one here.'

But the difference was, he had an ulterior motive. Revenge was the only reason he was expressing an in-terest in her. It wasn't as if he *wanted* to create a con-nection. In fact, it was the very last thing he intended to do. He'd probably find it easier to breathe and cool down if he stopped staring at her.

'I wonder where this pod is,' he mused, purposefully sliding his gaze from hers to look out to sea, even though it was a wrench.

'I hope we don't capsize when it comes along.'

'Why would we?' he said with a slight frown. 'This vessel is twenty metres long and five metres wide.'

'There's no need to be defensive. All I meant is that a blue whale can grow to more than that, certainly in length. The waves they generate from surfacing can be huge.'

'These are humpbacks.'

'Ah,' she said knowingly. 'They tend to be shorter, but they're restless and have a habit of investigating vessels. Let's hope they give us a wide berth.'

'Let's hope so.'

'So what do you find novel and appealing?' she asked, shifting slightly to face him, which dragged his gaze back to hers, as if their eyes were magnets.

Her. Sitting on his boat in the sunshine, looking as if she belonged there. But she didn't, no one did, so he scrubbed that thought from his head and drummed up a different answer. 'Swimming in new waters. Metaphorically speaking.'

'I thought you said it was just money.'

'It is. But having so much of it still requires some getting used to. Perhaps you could give me some tips.'

'I doubt it. The only thing I own personally is my flat in Athens and you've never needed any tips about anything, from what I recall.'

'Neither did you,' he said, thinking with a surge of heat about the way she'd instinctively known what turned him on most, right from the start. 'You always read me like a book. Remember Seville?'

She flushed. The pulse at the base of her neck fluttered madly. For a moment she appeared struck dumb. Was she doing as he suggested and remembering the weekend they'd taken things to another level? But then she swallowed hard and gave herself a quick shake. 'I was referring to your business and the articles I found on it.'

Oh. Right. 'Were you?'

'Absolutely,' she said coolly. 'Why on earth would you think otherwise?'

He didn't know. And come to think of it, that wasn't the only question he couldn't answer. Why did he feel as though he could sit here and talk to her for hours? Why did he want to grab her by the hand, take her down below and keep her there until neither of them could think straight? And why was he worried about the state of his boat and fascinated with the idea of sharing common ground with her when all that mattered was seducing and then abandoning her?

This expedition was not going the way he'd anticipated, he thought, his stomach churning with unease. He hadn't thought it through properly, or at all, if he was being honest. He was more on edge and less in control than he'd have liked. He had the horrible feeling that if he wasn't extremely careful he could wind up revealing more than he'd ever intended, which was less than zero, so he could not have been more relieved to suddenly spot a plume of water shooting up from the sea.

'Turn around,' he said, twisting abruptly to rummage in the hamper for the binoculars.

'Why?'

'Because we have company.'

Pacing up and down her balcony that night, not remotely soothed by the serenity of her room or the gentle sounds emanating from the tropical vegetation, Thalia reflected darkly that this afternoon's trip had been an extremely bad idea.

Not the actual whale-watching bit of it, of course. That had been incredible. She'd counted twelve animals in total. Eight adults, four calves. She'd never seen such magnificent creatures. They'd surfaced and hung around for over ten minutes before moving on, and she didn't mind admitting that the sight of the pod playing about in the water had stolen her breath and brought a tear to her eye.

Nor was Santi the cause of her woes. All he'd done was suggest an afternoon off, even if he had been irritatingly insistent about it.

No. What was really troubling her was, well, *her*. Or more precisely, her complete abandonment of common sense and resolve. She was the one who'd given in to temptation and agreed to go with him to see the whales, when she should have been stronger and resisted. She was the one who'd relaxed and lowered her guard, despite vowing to do precisely the opposite.

Why had she done all that? Had she gone mad? Honestly, she was hopeless. And she knew now that the whole adventure had been one colossal mistake because she was wound more tightly than the spring of the Rolex that circled her wrist.

If she'd been stronger and stayed behind, or even kept to the bow, as would have been sensible, she wouldn't have had a fascinating insight into his character or caught an intriguing glimpse of a possible inferiority complex, true. But nor would she have been plagued ever since with memories of their affair, thanks to his shocking and unexpected reference to it.

Seville.

How could she ever forget those two days, six weeks after they'd met? She'd been working in Madrid, he in Lisbon. They'd stayed in the marble-floored and stucco-walled presidential suite that occupied the entire top floor of the city's finest hotel. Through tall French doors, dressed with crisp white curtains, countless historic monuments beckoned, but they'd been ignored. In the master bedroom with its beige silk walls and subtle sense of glamour, he'd encouraged her out of her comfort zone for the first time. And, after taking to the new and exciting like a duck to water, she'd then pushed him out of his. Vanilla with a hint of chilli, was how she'd described the earth-shattering experience that had turned out to be not a one-off.

The arrival of the pod had provided a brief and stunning distraction but it had been over all too soon. And then, as Santi fired up the engine and motored them back—without dawdling, thank God—the memories had descended thick and fast and now she couldn't push them back into their box where they'd been kept under lock and key.

She couldn't help remembering the sex—how instinctively they'd moved together, how willingly they'd trusted each other and how white hot and intense the pleasure had been, whatever the spice. She couldn't stop thinking about what might have happened this afternoon had the wash of a whale rocked the boat and landed her in his arms. Nor could she forget how thrilling she'd found it when he'd sparked up a conversation with their fellow whale watchers in Portuguese, a language she didn't speak but perhaps ought to learn because it was so incredibly sexy, at least it was when he spoke it.

In his own environment, Santi was even more attractive than he was out of it. The desire that had been simmering away inside her for days was heating, which was a concern she'd feared even as far back as Saturday night, and she couldn't even find peace in sleep because jetlag was still keeping her awake. Her muscles ached. Her nerves were at snapping point. Her cortisol levels had to be stratospheric and, quite frankly, she didn't know how much more of it she could take.

Perhaps a swim and some exercise would provide the relief she needed, she thought in faint desperation, flapping a hand to dispatch a whining mosquito. Not here to relax, she hadn't packed a bikini, but she was hot and sticky and tingling all over. More importantly, it was the middle of the night and, while she might be wide awake, her infuriating host most likely was not.

Returning inside, Thalia grabbed a towel from the bathroom, carefully opened the bedroom door and peered into the soft darkness. She waited for a moment, ears pricked, then, encouraged by the silence, tiptoed out. She stealthily descended the floating staircase and headed to the pool, which shimmered enticingly beneath the silvery light of the moon that hung low and large in the inky sky.

Keen to feel the glide of cool water over her hot, sensitised skin, and yearning for the soothing of her turbulent thoughts, she dropped her towel on a lounger and quickly stripped off her camisole and shorts. She padded to the edge and was just about to slip silently in when from behind her came a dry, 'Nice evening for a dip.'

With a yelp of shock she lost her balance and her dignity and toppled in headfirst instead.

'What the hell do you think you're doing?' she spluttered once she'd surfaced, her heart thundering as she pushed her hair back, dashed water from her eyes and glared up at the man who was standing there looking tousled and disorientated. He wore nothing but a pair of close-fitting white shorts that left little to the imagination—not that she needed to use her imagination, because she knew exactly what lay beneath. 'You scared the living daylights out of me.'

'I could ask you the same thing,' he said gruffly. 'It's two-fifteen in the morning.'

'I still have jetlag.' And a bad case of Santi-itis to which she was *not* going to admit. 'I thought a swim might help. I had no idea you were awake.'

'I wasn't.'

'Then how did you know I was here? I was so quiet.'

'You set off the alarm.'

That would explain it. 'I wasn't aware there was one.'

'It's silent.'

'Sorry.'

'It's fine,' he said, shoving his hands through his hair and then rubbing them over his face in an obvious attempt to rouse himself properly.

But it wasn't fine, Thalia thought despairingly, the sight of his muscles doing their thing drawing her attention to his hard, hair-smattered torso and dissolving her stomach into a puddle of lust. Nothing about this situation was fine. In fact, it felt oddly intimate and decidedly dangerous and why, oh, why hadn't she just stayed upstairs and had a shower instead? 'Please turn around so I can get out.'

'I've seen you naked many times before.'

'That's completely irrelevant,' she said, flushing from head to toe despite the coolness of the water.

'Your rear view is as appealing as it ever was.'

Agh. He was utterly impossible. 'Are you going to do as I ask?'

'Why don't I join you instead?'

What? No. Absolutely not.

With the way she was feeling, who knew where skinny dipping with him might lead? The only solution was a speedy exit so she could recover and regroup and figure out how she was going to face him in the morning. If she was going to have to give him a full frontal now to achieve that, so be it.

Before she could question the wisdom of her decision, she pulled herself out of the pool, reached for the towel and wrapped it around her body. She picked up her sleepwear and was about to make a dash for the stairs, but then she made the mistake of casting him a quick glance. She instantly froze, because he was standing unexpectedly close, and something about the intensity with which he was looking at her switched every cell in her body to high alert.

She couldn't avert her gaze. She couldn't move. She just stood there, frozen, enveloped by the heat emanating off him and his intoxicating scent and drenched in pool water and want.

'I should go up,' she said, her voice so hoarse it was barely audible. 'I don't know what I was thinking. I apologise again for disturbing you. Goodnight.'

'Wait.'

Before she could take even one tiny step, his arm shot out and he wrapped his hand round her wrist, rooting her to the spot. Her skin burned where he touched her. The move closed the distance between them and altered the angle of their bodies. Now they stood almost chest to chest, and she could barely breathe.

His gaze dipped to her mouth and a bolt of desire shot through her, pooling low in her abdomen and firing heat through her veins. Time slowed right down and the world shrank. The air between them was heavy and crackling, as if a storm were about to break. She knew she ought to take a step back, shake him off and kill the buzz that she really didn't need, but she was gripped with such a strong urge to touch and taste that she could feel herself swaying towards him instead.

'What do you want?'

'You know what I want.' His voice was low, rough and scraped over her nerve endings.

'No,' she said, but her protest was weak.

'I've missed us, Thalia. It's been over a year since we broke up and despite how things ended, I still dream of you every night.'

Her head swam. She'd missed them and dreamed of him too. But she wasn't going to admit it. She'd already told him far too much. 'I don't.'

'I don't believe you.'

'Stop.'

'I can't. I don't how it's possible but you're more beautiful and sexier than ever. I look at you and I can remember every single extraordinary thing we did together as if it were yesterday. I want to pick up where we left off. Feel what you do to me.'

He gave her a gentle tug so their bodies were flush against each other. The hard length of his erection pressed into her abdomen and her heart crashed violently against her ribs. His mouth was mere inches from hers. She wanted to kiss it more than she'd ever wanted anything, to be instantly transported into a world where there was nothing but ecstasy.

'I can certainly feel what I do to you,' he murmured, stroking his thumb over the delicate skin of her wrist and the pulse there that was pounding wildly.

Denying it was pointless. Despite her words, her body was giving her away. Suddenly she couldn't remember why being with him here like this, now, wasn't a good idea, why she shouldn't be lifting her chin and setting her lips to his or sinking into a kiss with a soft sigh of longing and pleasure.

His mouth moved on hers slowly, thoroughly, and her head emptied of everything but him. Tiny flickering flames licked along her veins and desire swelled, an achingly sweet build-up of heat and need that robbed her of breath and liquefied her bones. Helplessly, she pressed herself closer, shifting against him to find some kind of relief for the aching throb between her legs, and the tempo of the kiss changed as it so often had in the past. He wrapped an arm around her waist—a band of steel that clamped her tight against him and prevented escape. Her free hand found its way to his neck and she dug her fingers into his hair, equally disinclined to let him go. The more he demanded from her, the hotter the fire in her belly burned. She wanted his hands all over her. She wanted him inside her with frenzied desperation.

'Come upstairs with me,' he murmured raggedly when he finally lifted his mouth from hers, and she was on the point of saying yes, yes, yes, when her conscience suddenly woke up and demanded to know what on earth she thought she was doing.

She froze. She gasped. Had she completely lost her mind? she wondered, appalled at her lapse of control, pulverised by excoriating heat and rampaging desire. However tempted she was, she could not go upstairs and make everything she'd dreamed of come true. She wouldn't succumb again. She would resist and reject him with everything she had, because her life right now had no space for any man, let alone one as wholly consuming and potentially damaging as him. She had to face reality, not escape it.

So she swallowed hard, took a deep breath and inched back to put some air between them. 'No,' she said, more breathlessly than she'd have liked.

'Why not?'

'Nothing can happen between us again. You know that. I even told you why.'

His eyes glittered in the low light. A muscle ticked in his jaw and his frown was deep. 'Do you still think you're better than me?'

What?

'Of course not,' she said with feeling. 'I never did. *You* thought that, and I have no idea where you got the idea from because what did I ever do to give you that impression?'

'You didn't correct it.'

'That you could think that of me hurt. Badly. I just wanted to leave to lick my wounds in private. I was referring to what I told you last night. But I have no wish to rehash the past, Santi, either the recent or the distant, even if you do. I'm here to work, and that's it.'

'Don't be naïve.'

'What do you mean?'

'You know as well as I do that you'll be in my bed before the week is out.'

Her breath caught and her heart lurched. She could see it. She wanted it. She didn't even find his arrogant presumption offensive. But he was wrong. Dead wrong. The kiss they'd just shared had been a moment of madness in the moonlight. Hell would freeze over before she fell back into his arms again. She was not as weak and vulnerable as she had been at the time of their affair. If, for some unfathomable reason, rekindling it had been his aim—with the flirting and the wandering about with very little on—he could forget it. She was never going to yield, and it was beyond time that he realised that.

'Sex isn't part of our deal,' she said, finally pulling herself free from his hold and ruthlessly stamping out the part of her that desperately wished it was. 'Your fifty million euros buy my time and expertise only. So if you think that sleeping with you is how I ought to be keeping you sweet, you can think again.'

CHAPTER SEVEN

SANTI WATCHED THALIA disappear back into the house for a moment, then spun round and dived into the pool. To clear his head. To rid his body of the desire that throbbed in every fibre of his being. To work out what the hell the last quarter of an hour had been about, because the one thing it *hadn't* been about was retribution.

Abruptly roused from a deep sleep, he had not been firing on all cylinders when he'd gone to investigate the security breach. He'd been hot, discombobulated and barely awake. Then he'd stumbled across Thalia in all her naked, beautiful, perfect glory and he'd instantly lost what little reason he had possessed.

She'd shimmered in the moonlight like some sort of nymph, all soft curves and long dark wavy hair. Every other memory of their short-lived affair—not just Seville, which had occupied his thoughts far too much this afternoon, and which he should never have brought up in the first place—had slammed into his head, one hot on the heels of the other, and instinct had taken over. He'd spoken nothing but the truth. He had dreamed of her. He did still want her, with a need that bordered on desperation.

But not for a single second had his plan for getting revenge and restoring control crossed his mind. He'd kissed her because after her bold and breathtaking exit from the pool he simply couldn't *not*. He'd invited her upstairs with no other thought in his head than getting her beneath him and sinking into her soft welcoming heat.

He should have kept his mouth shut. He knew from experience that if he'd focused on intensifying the kiss instead of suggesting they move things inside, he'd have had her flat on her back on a sun lounger within moments.

So why hadn't he? And why, when he could have easily salvaged the situation by kissing her again and relighting the fire, had he demanded an explanation for her refusal instead?

That had been an error. Demanding to know whether she still considered herself above him and exposing to her a vulnerability he barely admitted to himself had been another. And, come to think of it, why had his heart nearly leapt out of his chest when she'd fallen in the water in the first place?

He was more susceptible to her than he'd ever imagined, he thought grimly as he hit the end of the pool, turned and powered back down it. Physical involvement with her was obviously a must. Emotional involvement was very much a must not. Yet now, with her rejection of him smarting as if he'd been stung by a hornet, he was beginning to realise that ever since he'd laid eyes on her the night of the gala he was thinking and feeling things he shouldn't.

Take the strength of his reaction to events merely going his way. The triumph he'd felt when her lot had closed and he'd won. The relief when she'd showed up at the airport at nine a.m. on Sunday morning. The pleasure that had ripped through him at finally having her on his territory when she'd turned up here in a cloud of dust, irate and tired but still the most desirable woman he'd ever met. None of these outcomes had been a surprise, so why had he felt them so intensely?

Then there was the absurd and wholly unnecessary compulsion to impress her. When she'd boarded his plane and begun to question him about it he'd barely been able to stop himself from bragging. When she'd admired his house, he'd puffed up with pride. Asking for her opinion of her room had had him waiting for her answer with bated breath and, ridiculously, he had actually cared what she thought of the size of his boat. The moment he'd been turned away from his father's house without even the chance to show him what he'd made of himself he'd sworn never to try and impress anyone ever again. Yet when it came to Thalia he hadn't thought twice.

Not for a second since he'd switched tactics and knuckled down to work with her had he thought about using the fact that she badly needed his project to redress the balance of power between them. A word in the right ear and he could have destroyed her business before she even launched it. But instead, he'd immersed himself in the experience, basking in her enthusiasm and admiring her confidence. He'd looked forward to eight a.m. and willed the minutes to slow as six p.m. approached, and—his own discomfort and confusion aside—he'd enjoyed her excitement over the whales this afternoon far too much.

Lastly, and perhaps of the greatest concern, was how much he *did* dwell on everything she'd told him at supper the night before, despite his every intention not to. He wanted to have a word with Zoe about how Thalia felt, even though he didn't know her well enough for that level of intimacy and it was absolutely none of his business. He found himself contemplating sibling relationships, making unhelpful comparisons between his, which were non-existent, and hers, which were tricky but at least there, and then having to manage the resulting emotions. He was frequently preoccupied with the subject of her previous boyfriends, and he couldn't squash the annoyance that for her their affair had been nothing more than a displacement activity.

It couldn't continue. He had the sickening feeling that if he wasn't careful he could fall under her spell again and this time, instead of merely denting his pride and threatening his track record, she could do him serious damage.

He would not put himself in that position. He had no interest in emotions of a romantic nature. For years he'd been witness to the harm they could do. How often had he come home to find his mother in tears because his selfish, cruel father had casually cancelled a date? How much had he despised the way she rushed off to put on her best dress and a slash of red lipstick the minute she was summoned? Love was toxic, he'd come to realise. One party held all the cards, the other, none. It was a weakness that destroyed self-esteem and obscured reality.

It was now becoming blindingly clear that he'd been playing a dangerous game with Thalia. He'd allowed himself to be influenced by the past and had totally overreacted. Since when had he been so melodramatic? This wasn't some telenovela in which he had a starring role that demanded he avenge his mother's treatment at the hands of his father by taking it out on someone else. And how was he going to proceed anyway? Thalia's parting shot indicated a will that dominated chemistry, and that blew his plan to bits. Because how could he break up with her if he couldn't get her in the first place?

He'd been an idiot for thinking he had to resort to revenge to achieve his goals. Ejecting her from his life and drawing a line under the last sixteen months would be ample indication of the power and control he sought. That would be the act of a man ruled by cold calculation, not adolescent hot-headedness. And why did he care what she thought of him? What was so special about her? Nothing. Plenty of other people were glad of his company. Some were so desperate for it they didn't care where he and his money had come from.

His philanthropic intentions remained unchanged, but that posed no problem. He'd find another adviser somewhere at some point. Right now, however, the number one item on his agenda for the morning was sending his current adviser home.

CHAPTER EIGHT

'YOU'RE FIRING ME?'

Thalia stared at Santi from across her room just before eight the following morning, scarcely able to believe her ears. It had taken a lot of guts to answer his knock on the door. She couldn't think about the events of the night before without burning up with embarrassment and desire, but with so much at stake for her professionally, hiding beneath the sheets simply wasn't an option.

She'd brazen her way through the day by pretending it hadn't happened, she had figured as she'd showered and dressed. If at any point he referred to her nakedness or the kiss that had kept her awake for hours, she would take a leaf out of his book by simply ignoring it and changing the subject. She'd draw on all the deportment skills she'd learned at that ridiculous finishing school in Switzerland—which her mother had insisted she attend in a rare moment of maternal interest in her eldest daughter, but in hindsight hadn't been a complete waste of time—and focus on the work.

Not once had she envisaged that work being snatched away.

'Technically, I didn't hire you,' he said, standing in the doorway as still as a statue, his handsome face completely devoid of expression, his body language utterly unreadable, although the fact that he was fully dressed for once—in shorts, a buttoned-up shirt and deck shoes—didn't bode well. 'But essentially you are correct. I no longer require your services. The plane is still at the airfield. It will take you wherever you wish to go. It shouldn't take you long to pack.'

She stared at him, for a moment unable to convert her stunned thoughts into speech. *What on earth is going on?* she wondered, her head spinning like a top. He'd been so insistent she come here. He'd ruthlessly crushed her every attempt to push back, so a volte face like this made no sense at all. Unless the timing wasn't a coincidence and it was a direct response to their moonlit poolside encounter.

'Is this because I won't sleep with you?' she asked, chin up, eyes narrowed.

His jaw clenched, the tiniest indication that he wasn't quite as calm as he was trying to make out. 'Of course not.'

'Are you unhappy with my professional performance?'

'On the contrary.'

'Then why the sudden change of plan?'

His gaze dropped to her mouth and darkened. 'You mess with my head.'

'Yes, well, you mess with mine too,' she said, her

lips tingling while a shiver rippled down her spine. 'But for the sake of my career I'm prepared to rise above it.'

'Your career won't suffer,' he said flatly. 'I'll find you another project.'

'I don't want another project,' she shot back, equally prepared to dig her heels in. Because whatever he thought, she was not leaving. 'I'm already invested in yours and I'm enjoying it immensely. I've never started anything from scratch. This work is super-important to me and I intend to see it through to the end.'

'Too bad.'

It was for him. 'And let's not forget, you black-mailed me into coming here,' she felt obliged to point out. 'I rescheduled meetings and cancelled engage-ments to make this work. I've suffered swollen ankles and jetlag to accommodate your demands. I've danced to your tune for the last four days, and I will not risk my reputation and my future just because you can't control your response to me.'

'Leave and I'll donate another fifty million to the foundation.'

Ooh, that was a low blow. First blackmail, now bribery. It was a lot of money—and for a nanosecond she was torn—but she'd come this far and she was not for turning. And besides, she could match his offer any day of the week if she felt like it. 'I'm going no-where and you can't make me.'

His dark eyes flashed. 'Then *I'll* go.'

She blinked in shock. *What?* 'Where?'

'Anywhere.'

'Am I that much of a problem?'

'Yes.'

Wow. She didn't know whether she was flattered or outraged. 'You'd really leave me here on my own?'

'Absolutely,' he confirmed with a sharp nod. 'The kitchen is very well stocked and my housekeeper can be put on standby if needs be. You have a car and you're not without other resources.'

All of that was true, yet he clearly wasn't thinking straight because this was completely nuts. 'You're overreacting.'

'The situation as it stands is untenable. It has to come to an end. But don't worry, I'll give you an excellent reference.'

She didn't care about the reference. Well, not right now she didn't. She cared about improving literacy and helping kids out of the favelas and launching his charity and her business with a bang. But more than that, she and Santi weren't done. Not by a long shot. Quite why this was the case when she had no intention of kissing him again she had no idea, but she felt it in her bones. By hook or by crook she would resolve this situation to her satisfaction, which was why, when he spun on his heel and strode out of the room, she scooted round the bed in hot pursuit of him.

'Now hang on a minute,' she said, hurrying to catch him up as he crossed the deck as if he had the hounds of hell snapping at his feet. 'Why is the situation untenable? I'm sure we can find a suitable compromise. Wait. Santi. This simply isn't—'

But she didn't get to finish her sentence because

the next second she'd tripped over a low-level branch, her ankle had twisted and given way and she was crashing to the floor. On landing, she let out a howl of pain and cursed loudly and fluently the architectural oddities of this house that meant it had trees growing inside it.

Santi stopped abruptly, whipped round and stalked back to her. 'Did you do that deliberately?'

Now she *was* outraged. 'Of course I didn't,' she snapped as she sat up, gingerly prodded her ankle and gritted her teeth against the sharp pain that shot up her leg. 'You need to get an arborist in here. This whole place is ridiculous.'

'When you grow up in the sort of place I did, greenery matters.'

'That's what a garden's for.'

'Let me take a look.'

'I'm fine.'

Ignoring her, he bent down, scooped her up into his arms and dumped her on the chair in which, thirty-six hours earlier, she'd stupidly revealed her issues with her brother and her identity. While she fought for breath and control of her spinning head, he dropped to a squat, lifted her foot onto his knee and slid off her shoe.

'Does that hurt?' he asked, pressing his fingers against the tender bump that was rapidly swelling around the bone.

'Ouch,' she muttered with a wince. 'Yes.'

'What about this?'

He gently rotated her foot and brought tears to her eyes. 'On a scale of one to ten, it's an eleven.'

'I'll sort out some ice and then get the first aid kit.'

'I thought you had a plane to catch.'

His jaw was tight. His mouth was set in a flat line, frustration radiating off him in waves. And even though she really hadn't tripped on purpose, she was glad his plans had been thwarted. Now he knew what it felt like.

'Evidently not any more.'

Santi vented his feelings about this infuriating turn of events by filling the air with muttered expletives while he rummaged around in the bathroom for a tubular support bandage and painkillers. He'd had it all mapped out. All sorted. But Fate had clearly had other ideas and what the hell else could he do? He could hardly leave Thalia here on her own with an ankle that was swollen and sore but thankfully appeared to be sprained rather than broken. Yes, he was keen to remove himself from her head-wrecking orbit so he could forget about her and the damn kiss that had kept him up all night, but he wasn't completely without empathy.

He should have waited until she appeared downstairs at eight before confronting her, he thought grimly, finally finding what he was looking for. That would have been a root-free event. But it would also have meant firing her by the pool, the scene of the crime, and the last thing he'd wanted was to recall the unacceptable madness that had happened there beneath the moonlight. Besides, regret was pointless. Grudgingly admitting she was right about the need to hire a tree surgeon served no purpose at all. A solution to the situation was what was required.

As he stalked off in search of a pair of crutches— souvenirs of a broken tibia he'd suffered while skiing in St Moritz a couple of years ago—he figured he'd just have to follow her example and rise above the attraction. He didn't have any other choice. He'd immerse himself in the tasks he'd set her and keep face-to-face interaction to a minimum. As much as he was able to he would steer clear of her, and when he couldn't he'd simply ignore her scent, her gaze, her presence, her everything. It needn't be for long. It had once amused and suited him to keep her around indefinitely but that was very much not the case now. He wanted her out of his house as soon as was practicably possible, and he'd do everything in his power to facilitate that.

Laden with medical equipment, Santi headed back to his inconvenient patient. He set the crutches to one side, braced himself, then resumed his position at her feet.

'You wanted the ten days to run consecutively?' he muttered, removing the ice he'd packed around the swelling and observing with some relief that at least it hadn't got any bigger. 'You have them. In fact, why don't we take the day we flew here as day one? We've completed two more since then, so another week and we'll be done. Your ankle should be healed by then. And on that note we'll revert to your original idea of working up here. No need to navigate the stairs and risk further injury.'

And no unnecessary torment caused by memories of last night by the pool either.

'Oh,' she said dully. 'OK.'

Expecting more enthusiasm for the idea and not a little gloating, due to the fact that he was giving her her way on a number of fronts, Santi glanced up at her and frowned. She looked shaken and distressed, he noted with a sudden skip of his pulse and a sharp squeeze of his chest. Was she in a lot of pain? Could she be going into shock? How on earth would he treat that? He raked his gaze over her a little more intently and saw with alarm that she was trembling.

'Is everything all right?' he said, concerned that the painkillers and a stretchy bandage might not cut it and vaguely wondering where the nearest hospital might be. 'You're very pale. Do you need to lie down?'

Thalia blinked slowly, as if coming out of a trance, and gave herself a quick shake. 'What? No. I'm fine,' she said with the flash of a smile that didn't quite reach her eyes and did little to reassure him. 'Everything's fine.'

'Are you sure?'

'Absolutely.'

She sounded adamant even if she looked anything but. He'd have to take her word for it and keep a close watch over her. 'Let me know immediately if that changes.'

'Of course.'

* * *

But while Santi had been fetching the first aid kit and crutches, Thalia had received a phone call from Atticus, and as a result of it, nothing was fine at all.

When she'd seen his name flash up on the screen she'd thought, with an absurd little bubble of hope and delight, that perhaps he'd telepathically felt her pain and was ringing to see if she was all right. He wasn't, of course. He hadn't felt her pain for many months now.

'Hey, sis,' he'd said in Greek from down the other end of the line—in Naxos, she'd presumed, although the days of him letting her know where he was all the time were long gone. 'I have some news. Zoe's pregnant.'

It was a good thing she'd been sitting down because she'd suddenly felt as if she were falling from a great height. A lead weight had seemed to settle on her chest, compressing her lungs and making it hard to breathe. 'Oh, wow,' she'd managed brightly, her throat tight, her heart thumping oddly fast. 'Congratulations.'

'It's three months now. All's going well.'

'I'm so pleased.'

'Would you like me to send you a copy of the ultrasound?'

Not particularly. She didn't need physical proof that their lives were spinning off in even more divergent directions. But what sort of a sister would she be to say thanks but no thanks? Envy and resentment were terrible emotions to experience at such a happy announcement, and very few sets of twins celebrated life's milestones at the same time. So she'd taken a deep steadying breath, fixed a smile to her face in the hope that it would be reflected in her voice and said, 'Very much.'

'I'll email it over now.'

'Do the others know?'

'You're the first I've told.'

Some consolation…

'But Willow guessed a couple of weeks ago,' Atticus had continued, killing that tiny buzz stone dead. 'The four of us went for dinner and she noticed that Zoe wasn't drinking or eating shellfish. She teased out the truth.'

Oh.

'I'm so pleased,' she'd said again, finding it hard to speak around the hot tight lump in her throat. 'Please say hi to Zoe and pass on my congratulations.'

'I will.'

At the other end of the line, she'd heard a muffled voice and then Atticus had said, 'I'd better go,' and cut the call, leaving her awash with emotion and floundering until Santi had returned with the supplies to fix her ankle.

Thalia tried not to mind that her brother hadn't even asked how she was, let alone where she was, what she was doing and who she was doing it with. It might have been nice to have been the first to know about the baby beyond their little unit of two, but just because she was Atticus's twin it wasn't her *right*. And it was natural that he and Zoe would meet up with

Leo, their eldest brother, and his wife. Why wouldn't they double date? They were the perfect foursome.

She was thrilled for her brother and sister-in-law. Of course she was. But God she was lonely. She'd attended so many weddings recently. Three of them had involved her siblings. Everyone seemed to be coupling up but her. She was thirty-one. She'd always wanted to get married and have a family of her own, despite the train wreck of her parents' union and the terrible example they'd set. Sometimes she yearned for it so much her heart physically ached, even though she'd had to put men on pause while she completed this journey of self-discovery.

So why couldn't she find her soulmate? Was it simply that not knowing who she was doomed a relationship from the start? Or did she expect too much? Was she so used to the close connection she'd had with Atticus that she subconsciously sought a similarly intense and instant connection with the men she dated? Could that also be why they failed? Because she had little time for superficiality and small talk and threw in the towel too soon?

She'd certainly had an intense and instant connection with Santi, she thought, watching him stretch the bandage over her foot with his lovely, big, capable hands, the pain of the sprain lessening as she began to suffuse with heat. And not just a physical one. They hadn't talked all that much or all that deeply during their torrid twelve-week affair, but it was uncanny how often, when they were apart, she'd be daydreaming about him and a message would arrive in her inbox or on her phone a second or two later. Whatever the content—a logistical arrangement, an amusing anecdote about work, a spot of sexting—they'd always perked her up, she recalled.

So maybe he could perk her up now.

And maybe she should let him.

Because, actually, why *was* she fighting the attraction? Did giving in to it and losing herself in the blissful pleasure that only he could give her *really* have to be a problem? The circumstances of this situation didn't remotely resemble that of their affair. For one thing, now he'd agreed to the consecutiveness of their workdays—an unexpected yet satisfying solution to the stalemate they been stuck at before she'd tripped—her stay here had a deadline. So there simply wouldn't be time for things to get complicated. And she was so much stronger now. The chances of being blown off course again were virtually non-existent.

She wanted him desperately. Instead of constantly battling the desire, she longed to embrace it and let it flow. She wanted more of the kisses that led to long hot nights of fireworks and oblivion. It would be beneficial to rid herself of the unbearable tension that was causing her so much stress, she told herself. She would be more productive and better able to do her job. And would it not give her a form of closure?

'Why are you looking at me like that?' Santi muttered, jolting her out of her thrilling, tumbling thoughts.

'How am I looking at you?'

'As if you're thinking about kissing me.'

Her gaze dropped to his gorgeous mouth and lingered. Her pulse rate accelerated as shivers began to race up and down her spine. 'What if I am?'

His hands stilled on her foot. 'Did you bang your head when you tripped?' he said with a frown.

'No.'

'Then why?'

'Because I'm tired of fighting the attraction I feel for you,' she confessed, lifting her eyes to his, but finding nothing to read in their dark unfathomable depths. 'I don't think I can stand another seven days of it. I accused you of overreacting before, but it's entirely possible I've been guilty of the same.'

'I understood I'd be an unwelcome distraction.'

'You wouldn't be unwelcome any more. Why don't you kiss me again and see?'

He shook his head and returned his attention to his doctoring. 'It's not going to happen.'

'Why not?'

'You might have changed your mind, but I haven't. If you hadn't sprained your ankle, I'd be long gone.'

'But surely if we want each other the situation is no longer untenable.'

'I don't want you.'

She didn't believe that for a second. He might not want to want her, but he had last night. Very much. 'It would be just sex,' she said, focusing on getting what she needed instead of the turmoil in her head and the trouble in her heart. 'For six nights. That's all I ask.'

'You're not having it. Think of the damage sleeping with a client would do to your reputation.'

'Who needs to know?' He wouldn't tell. He hadn't said a word about their affair. 'You even said I'd be in your bed before the week was out.'

'I was mistaken.'

'Do you really think you'll be able to resist me?'

'Without a shadow of a doubt.'

'You couldn't before.'

'That was then.'

Yes, well, they'd soon see about that.

CHAPTER NINE

ONCE HER ANKLE was securely bound, Santi left Thalia to make her own way to the workspace that she'd identified as suitable the morning after she'd arrived. To help her there he'd have to touch her in places that were more tantalising and dangerous than a lower leg—the handling of which had been a tough test of his willpower as it was—and she had the crutches. Arranging a stool with a cushion upon which to rest her foot was as far as he was prepared to go and, having done that, he removed to the kitchen to prepare breakfast. He took his time over it, because eggs and fruit should not be rushed, he felt, then delivered the tray to the table at which she now sat and stalked off.

'Wait. Where are you going?' she called after him, sounding faintly startled and not a little aggrieved.

Anywhere she wasn't, he thought darkly. Just because the out-of-sight-out-of-mind theory hadn't worked thirteen months ago, it didn't mean it wouldn't now. 'Downstairs.'

'What if I need something?'

'Call me.'

He descended the stairs two at a time and strode

into his ground floor study, resolutely not thinking about kissing her or her shockingly tempting proposal. But he'd barely had time to fire up his laptop before his phone rang.

'So sorry to disturb you so soon,' she said, practically purring down the line, 'but would you be an angel and bring me some sparkling water?'

Gritting his teeth, Santi told himself that it was his own damn fault he was in this position. Thalia had injured herself at his home and was in pain because of him—again. Although physically this time rather than emotionally, and at least that could be alleviated with medication. Therefore he'd fetch her her water.

Ten minutes later, he was summoned to adjust the stool. A quarter of an hour after that, he had to go and check that the bandage wasn't too tight because she couldn't feel her toes, and five minutes after *that* he brought his laptop back upstairs and plonked it down at the other end of the table because all this toing and froing was driving him nuts.

The rest of the morning passed achingly slowly. Ostensibly he researched literacy programmes, but in reality he was so distracted that he achieved very little. Her gaze kept sliding in his direction and lingering—as intense, as focused and as sizzling as a laser. She claimed his attention on the most spurious of pretexts and, once she had it, she batted her eyelashes at him and smiled winningly, all wide-eyed innocence and sultry seductiveness, which was a truly mind-boggling combination.

'It's fascinating to see you in your natural habitat,'

she mused at one point as if he were a wild animal, which was apt, given how he was beginning to feel.

'Is it?' he replied, feigning a complete lack of interest in her observation and keeping his focus on the screen of his laptop.

'You suit this environment far more than any one of the hotels rooms we frequented.'

'Are you implying I lack elegance and sophistication?'

She was silent for a moment as if she was considering that, and then she said, 'Not exactly. Although those wouldn't be the adjectives I'd use to describe you.'

'Which ones would you use?'

'Untamed. Unpredictable. Unbelievably exciting.'

The first two certainly applied to him now. She'd mentioned the hotel rooms and all he could think was the heat they'd found in them, the passion and then, God, the boundary pushing that she'd embraced with an enthusiasm that he suspected had destroyed him for anyone else. 'You never seemed to mind that.'

'Oh, I don't mind at all.'

She clearly saw his refusal to engage in a six-night fling with her as a challenge, the irony of which did not escape him. But he could handle a few smouldering looks, a smattering of barely-there touches that nevertheless set him on fire, and the occasional reference to their affair, he assured himself as he did his utmost to ignore her. He couldn't control her behaviour, but he could most certainly control his. He would not forget the danger she presented and he would not take her up on her proposition, no matter how great the attack on his defences, which she upped after lunch.

She was on the phone, rattling away in French to a lawyer who apparently specialised in global charities, when a parcel with her name on it was delivered to the house. Refusing his offer of help, she hobbled with it to her room. Twenty minutes later she emerged, having swapped her usual uniform of smart trousers and demure top for a skimpy black bikini and a pink and gold sarong. Her hair was down, instead of up, flowing loose over her shoulders, and at the shocking, gorgeous sight of her Santi nearly swallowed his tongue.

But he did not comment. Not when she made her way back across the deck, her barely confined breasts jiggling with every hop of the crutches. Not when she sat down and adjusted her bikini top, which surely didn't need to take nearly as long as it apparently did. Not even when she shot him a heat-filled glance and fluffed out her hair—just as she'd used to after they'd had sex—did he react.

He would not give her the satisfaction of knowing how much she affected him. How very un-angelic the thoughts stampeding through his head were. She would not win this battle of attrition she'd decided to wage. All he had to do was stay strong, maintain his grip on his control and count down the minutes until he could put her on a plane.

But in the event, despite his very best efforts, her assault on him proved so effective that his defences didn't even make it past seven before collapsing into rubble.

'I'm clocking off,' she said on the dot of six p.m. 'Would you mind carrying me down to the pool? I could really do with a swim.'

Yes, he did mind, he thought, his jaw tight, every muscle in his body tensing. Very much. It had been bad enough picking her up when she'd tripped, but at least then she'd been clothed. All that soft warm semi-naked flesh in his arms now might just undo him as it had done last night.

'The bandage isn't waterproof,' he said, sounding as though he'd swallowed rocks.

'Then I'll take it off.'

That made him envisage her taking everything else off too, and he remembered how she'd looked in the moonlight until he ruthlessly obliterated the images from his head. 'If you so wish.'

'Please?'

The bat of the eyelashes and the tremulous smile bounced straight off his armour. They didn't suit her anyway. 'No.'

'I'm not sure trying to make it down the stairs with crutches on my own would be a good idea. As you pointed out earlier, there might be a risk of further injury.'

And *she'd* accused *him* of manipulation? 'That's why there's a handrail,' he said flatly. 'One on each side. Take it slowly. You'll be fine.'

She gave a deep sigh of resignation. 'All right,' she said with overly dramatic despondency. 'I guess I can manage.'

She got up awkwardly and made her way with

apparent difficulty to the stairs. Abandoning the crutches, she grasped the handrail and took a step. She immediately went rigid, and her breath hissed through her teeth, and with a clatter of his chair Santi sprang to his feet.

'Oh, for God's sake,' he muttered, very nearly at the end of his tether as he strode towards her. Whether or not she was faking it, he couldn't let this continue. What if she fell? Did he want that on his conscience too? And why the bloody hell hadn't he had a lift installed?

He grabbed her free arm and wound it round his neck with one hand and planted the other on her waist. 'Lean on me.'

'Thank you.'

Together they made their way down the stairs, and as he huffed and grunted he wondered if she really needed to lean into him quite so closely? He could smell the shampoo she used, and memories of all the showers and baths they'd shared slammed into his head. The minimalist slate bathroom that had a panoramic view of the Tokyo skyline and a bath that comfortably fit two... The South African game reserve treehouse with its open-air bedroom and the glassed-in shower around which a thunderstorm had raged... The smooth softness of her skin beneath his fingers made him think of the endless hours he'd spent exploring her body with his hands and his mouth in all four corners of the globe and he ached to do it again.

At the bottom of the stairs, in order to put a swifter end to his torment, Santi swept Thalia up into his arms once more and strode across the grass to the pool area, avoiding with determination the pool itself and targeting a double sun lounger instead. He deposited her in the centre of it, wondering if he would ever be able to scrub from his head the feel of all that warmth and softness plastered up against him. He was about to spin round and make a bid for freedom, for air, for sanity, when she suddenly whipped off her bikini top and all the blood shot from his head to his groin.

'I thought you were going for a swim,' he growled, frozen to the spot, his scowl so fierce he suspected it might well turn permanent.

'I think I'll sunbathe for a bit first.' She looked up at him, her eyes lit with a wicked gleam that triggered a surge of desire so overwhelming it threated to swamp him. She waved a hand in the direction of her chest. 'You aren't bothered by a bit of toplessness, are you? You did say you'd seen it all before.'

He had said that and he had seen it all before. But this was different. Now he didn't want to see any-thing. Except, he did. *Por Deus*, he *did*. He wanted to look at her for hours and touch her and taste her so badly he was in agony, and when she wriggled back to make herself comfortable, what remained of his control evaporated.

What was his problem? he wondered as the final strand of his stretched-to-the-limit patience snapped. Why was he making such a mountain out of this molehill? He hadn't slept with anyone in the thirteen months since they'd split up—even the thought of it had made him recoil with distaste—so he should be biting her hand off. It was just sex, until she left. Six nights of the extraordinarily intense pleasure he'd only experienced with her.

What damage could she possibly do in that time? There'd be no risk of emotional involvement. The only thing they'd be sharing was the incredible passion that burned between them, which ought to be indulged because it was so staggeringly rare. He would never be lured from the purely physical. Of that he was absolutely certain. So what was he worried about? And did it really matter who was in control right now?

'I give up,' he said, lowering himself to the lounger, his pulse hammering and his entire body racked with anticipation. 'You win.'

'I don't know what you're talking about.'

'Yes, you do.'

'You're right,' she said, an almost beatific smile curving her beautiful mouth as he leaned in, planting his hands either side of her, and she fell back. 'I absolutely do.'

Oh, thank God for that, Thalia thought, wrapping her arms around Santi's neck and almost weeping with relief as his mouth came down on hers. He'd put up quite a fight. She'd had to pull out all the stops. For one heart-stuttering moment she'd thought she'd failed, and the rejection that had sliced through her had been twice as sharp as anything she'd felt this morning on the phone to Atticus. But then his resistance had visibly disintegrated and now he was kissing her with a thousand times more heat and passion than he had done last night.

Losing herself in the electrifying sensations shooting through her, from the top of her head to the tips of her toes, she moaned and tangled her fingers in his hair. The kiss turned harder and wilder, and with what few functioning brain cells she had left she wondered whether he sought to punish her for her games. But if he did, he was failing. She wanted it all, whatever he had in mind for her.

She tightened her hold on him, just in case he had any intention of pulling away—which would be punishment indeed—and with a harsh groan, he moved a hand to her hip. He slid it up her side until he reached her breast and she instinctively arched her back in encouragement, craving the full contact that she knew from experience would be thrilling, but to her frustration he refused to comply.

'Touch me properly,' she panted, wrenching her mouth from his to catch her breath, willing to beg if she had to.

'When I'm ready,' he said roughly, his voice gravelly and low. 'I'm the one in control now.'

'Tease.'

'You're one to talk.'

Her head spinning, her heart pummelling her ribs, she pressed on his shoulders to urge him lower. But all he did in response was reach for her wrists and trap them in one hand above her head against the lounger. The other he skimmed over her body with featherlight caresses that made her whimper and shiver and writhe.

The torment was relentless, the tension unbearable. He trailed kisses all over her neck and finally gave her what she needed by cupping her breast with one big warm hand. Within moments she couldn't take any more. She was burning up, needing release, and she drew in a ragged breath to plead with him when he deftly undid the knot tying her sarong. Then he dipped his hand beneath the band of her bikini bottoms and the words dried up in her throat. He captured her achingly tight nipple in his mouth and eased his fingers into her slick wet heat, and she had to bite on her lip to stop herself from crying out at the intensity of the pleasure that whirled through her.

He knew exactly what drove her wild. He'd once dedicated hours to finding out and he hadn't forgotten a thing. He showed her no mercy. He wound her tighter and drove her higher and he didn't stop until she was trembling and moaning and shattering beneath him as fireworks exploded behind her eyelids and wave upon wave of ecstasy thundered over her.

'Are you still on the pill?' he said hoarsely some minutes later.

His words were muffled by the fog in her head and the pounding of her pulse as she floated down to earth. All she could manage was a weak shake of the head and a soft, breathless, 'No need.'

'So you haven't been dating all that much, then?'

'No.'

'Don't go anywhere.'

There was no chance of that. She couldn't have moved even if she'd wanted to. Her limbs had lost all strength. Her bones had dissolved. She was still seeing stars. Had it always been that intense? Or had the build-up of tension over the last four days after such a long absence added a dimension that hadn't existed before?

Tiny aftershocks of pleasure rippled through her. She touched the tips of her fingers to her abdomen and the muscles beneath her skin twitched. Incredibly, she could feel desire stirring again. She closed her eyes, flattening her hand and inching it down her body, imagining his mouth there, on her, as he—

'Stop that.'

Her eyes flew open and her hand stilled, her entire being flooding with heat at being caught in the act—even though it was nothing she hadn't done before with him. 'What took you so long?'

His mouth quirked. 'How's the sprain?'

'What sprain?'

'Very funny.'

'I can't feel a thing.'

'That'll be the endorphins.'

'I think I need more.'

'I'll see what I can do.'

He took care removing her bikini bottoms. Less so tossing them to the ground. He pulled his T-shirt over his head and that joined them. His shorts and underwear followed a second later but she didn't have time to ogle the magnificence of his body because, barely before she had time to think—*hello!*—he'd rolled on a condom with more dexterity than she could have managed, given how badly she was shaking, and settled himself between her thighs.

He kissed her deeply and lengthily, until the world faded away and there was only this. Only him. She ran her hands over his shoulders, loving the feel of his muscles flexing, and then over his hot smooth back and lower.

They'd done this so many times, she thought giddily, yet each time had been a revelation. Now was no different. She could sense an urgency in him she'd never felt before. And a restraint. Because of her ankle? It genuinely didn't hurt. She raised the leg in question and wrapped it around his hips, bending the knee of the other, instinctively lifting her pelvis to hurry him along. As ever he read her body beautifully. In one easy move he pushed into her, and the feel of him hard and deep inside her was so achingly familiar—as if it had been days since he'd been there, not months—that she found she had to swallow down a tiny lump in her throat.

Santi swore gutturally, suggesting he was equally affected. Then he began to move, his breath hot and harsh on her neck, his delicious weight pressing her down, and she could do no more than just close her eyes and go with it.

While he transported her to a place where there was nothing but the promise of explosions and oblivion she dug her fingers into his hair and clung on. She pressed hot kisses to his neck and nipped his earlobe and felt the shudders rip through him. He cupped a breast and rubbed a thumb over her nipple. Her heart nearly leapt out of her chest. And all the while, he thrust in and out of her, the thrillingly exciting friction there and everywhere else obliterating her reason, her thoughts, everything but her senses.

The tension spiralling inside her was maddening. She was prickling all over, hurtling towards a destination she knew from experience was star-filled and wondrous, and she wanted to get there. She wanted to get there so desperately. Her blood was boiling. Her nerve endings were on fire. Murmured words flowed from her mouth in broken incoherent bursts, about how good he was making her feel, what she wanted him to do to her and what she was going to do to him later.

In response, he quickened and deepened his movements, and crushed his mouth to hers in an earth-shattering kiss that propelled the tingling in her toes up through her body, spreading into every inch of her with ever increasing intensity, until it split her apart, drenching her in pleasure and wrenching his name from her lips.

While she trembled and gasped, he held her tight and then buried himself in her one last time, so deep it was as if he wanted to fuse himself to her. With a muffled roar, he climaxed, pulsing into her so fiercely that it detonated another mini explosion, and then he collapsed on top of her.

And as their breathing evened, and their heartbeats slowed, Thalia lay beneath him, slightly squashed, slightly sweaty, her ankle now beginning to throb a little. But her head was blissfully empty and her troubling feelings were soothed, and there really was no place she'd rather be.

CHAPTER TEN

SEVERAL HOURS LATER, in his bed, to which he'd carried Thalia when the sun had set and a chill had tinged the air, Santi peeled himself away from her and flopped onto his back in order to recover from the latest in a long line of mind-blowing orgasms. He was boneless, blissed out and overcome with lassitude. He might have lost today's battle down there by the pool, he thought woozily, as his body cooled and his surroundings swam back into focus, but it didn't feel much like defeat.

'Why did we ever stop doing this?' he murmured absently once he'd regained the power of speech, rolling onto his side and propping himself up on an elbow.

Evidently less affected than he was by the sex marathon they'd just undergone, Thalia sat up abruptly, clasping the sheet to her chest, and stared at him wide-eyed and open-mouthed. 'Are you serious?' she said with a quick fluff of her gloriously tousled hair. 'You broke us up.'

'You did that,' he corrected. 'I just got there first.'

'With wholly unfounded and hurtful accusations,' she said, looking still ever so slightly upset about it.

'I'll never forget them. You called me a pampered princess. You said my nose was stuck so high in the air it was a wonder I could see where I was going. That I wouldn't know real life even if I were stripped of everything I had and dumped right in the middle of it. Why did you even *say* those things?'

Santi winced, his gut churning with self-recrimination as he remembered the conversation. Her question was one he didn't particularly want to answer. At least, not with the truth. His burning need for control and where it stemmed from was a rabbit hole down which he would never venture with her. He rarely went down it himself. He didn't like to recall the teenage rage and resentment he'd felt at his father's rejection and his mother's despair, or how hard he'd found it to contain those emotions and stay on track. If it hadn't been for the intervention and mentorship of a charity-organised youth worker—who'd met him when he was fourteen soon after his friend had been killed, and had introduced him to literacy, computers and coding—he could have easily gone down an altogether different path.

He should never have brought the matter up, he thought regretfully. If Thalia hadn't rendered him so weak and befuddled he'd have been more circumspect. He'd have to take more care going forward.

But perhaps he ought to apologise for the things he'd said to her that morning. She'd had the courage to explain where she'd been at the time and he'd reluctantly come to realise that he could have been wrong about the icy disdain she'd bestowed on him.

It might not have been a reaction to him but rather to what he'd said. And this was the second time she'd sought clarification. Even if he had had the energy to distract her by kissing her until she couldn't think about anything other than him, continued avoidance did rather smack of cowardice.

'You caught me by surprise and I don't take rejection well,' he said, as if it had really been that simple.

'Who does?' she observed with a frown. 'But all I'd said was that we needed to talk.'

'Everyone knows what that means, and I was right, wasn't I?'

'That's still no excuse for lashing out the way you did.'

'I know. I handled it badly. I apologise.'

She tilted her beautiful head and regarded him quizzically. 'Was I ever arrogant or condescending towards you?'

'No.'

'I don't even know why you thought I would be. I mean, I'm not generally. I'm acutely aware of how lucky I've been and how privileged I am. And why on earth would anyone look down on you with everything you've achieved?'

Which was what, exactly? A stuffed bank account and a private jet? A formidable reputation in the business world and stellar success? It would never have been enough.

He could still recall turning up at his father's sprawling villa in Copacabana, shortly after he'd set up his software business and sold his first licence, thinking that finally he'd done something to make the old man proud enough to recognise him and welcome him into his life. Only to have the housekeeper shut the door in his face. Now the guy had been dead for eight years and he'd never be impressed.

'I wasn't ready for us to be over,' he said, stifling the troublesome memories and the unpleasant emotions that they stirred up. 'It was a cheap shot to save face. I'm sorry I hurt you. That was never my intention.'

'You should have let me explain.'

Perhaps she was right, but ultimately there'd have been little point. It wouldn't have changed anything. It wasn't as if he'd have offered to help her with what she'd been going through. He didn't have the necessary resources, and emotional support had never been—and never would be—his thing. Although if he had heard her out he could have avoided hurting her, he supposed. 'The result would have been the same.'

'But not the fallout. Thanks to you I spent weeks fretting over everyone I'd ever met and everything I'd ever said to them. What with all the other angst I had going on at the time, my confidence had already taken a battering. You demolished what was left of it. It's been hard work getting it back.'

Great shafts of guilt swiped at his conscience. He hadn't thought about her at all. That morning had been all about him. If only he hadn't fallen into old bad habits the repercussions would have been different for him too. He could have avoided the strange ache he'd felt deep inside in the days after their breakup.

He wouldn't have stewed in a swamp of familiar resentment and perceived injustice these last thirteen months. He'd have had no need for retribution. She wouldn't be here now.

Something twanged in his chest and he rubbed it away. 'How can I make it up to you?' he said, not wanting to analyse quite how he felt about her not being here and instead switching his focus from the past to the present.

'You can start by making me something to eat.'

While Santi took himself off to heat up some delicious-sounding fish stew that his housekeeper had prepared earlier, Thalia downed two painkillers, arranged a cushion to support her ankle and contemplated his recent confession.

Obviously she was delighted they'd finally cleared up the Paris misunderstanding, but she did get the feeling that there had to be more to his explanation than met the eye. Such impulsivity didn't fit with the man who'd built a successful business from scratch and sold it for billions at the relatively young age of thirty-four. He couldn't have done that with a thin skin. He'd have failed at the first hurdle. So he must have developed inches-thick armour plating. He must also have faced rejection many times over.

But perhaps not on a personal level, it occurred to her as she settled back against a pile of pillows and awaited his return. Because who in their right mind would ever voluntarily ditch a gorgeous, successful man like him? If she hadn't had an exceptionally good reason for doing so, she certainly wouldn't have. She'd never met anyone who'd got her quite so well quite so quickly. They might not have talked in much depth during their affair, but the messages they'd sent each other had been frequent—dozens of mini conversations that had kept her going when they'd been apart—and excitement had leapt inside her on receipt of every single one. There'd been no thoughts of throwing in the towel with him. The three months they'd dated was the longest she'd ever been out with anyone. Who knew what might have happened if they'd met at another time?

No doubt, when it came to relationships, he was used to being the dumper rather than the dumpee, and it was his fragile male ego that had pushed him to jump in before she could say anything. But now she was wondering why he remained single despite having everything going for him. Did he have commitment issues? His father had never featured in his life. He hadn't even known who he was, she'd read. So could that be it? He had no example to follow? It didn't seem the most likely explanation. Her parents' marriage had been deeply dysfunctional—how they managed to produce six children she had no idea— but that didn't stop her from wanting a partner and family of her own.

So maybe he just hadn't met the right woman. In fact, who *would* be the right woman? The dates he'd had in the past, according to photos in the press—and she'd cast only a very casual eye over them—suggested he didn't have a type. Not that she was interested or anything. All she wanted from him was a successful outcome for his project and mind-blowing sex for a week. She didn't have the time or the head space for anything more.

But maybe she ought to investigate a little deeper and push a little harder when she ventured into more personal waters and he inevitably changed the subject. She ought to know more about the man she was going to be sleeping with for the next six nights. She was no longer prepared to let him get away with shutting her down the minute she got too close.

She knew it wouldn't be easy. He was harder to crack than the most sophisticated of safes. But by his own admission he owed her and she would prevail. Somehow, she would lull him into a false sense of security with so much sex it would turn his brain to mush and then—bam!—she'd unlock all his secrets and have him right where she wanted him.

The following morning, citing expediency—easy elevation of her still slightly swollen ankle, a convenient location to indulge the attraction whenever it overtook them—Santi convinced Thalia to work from the bed. She needed no persuasion and twenty-four hours later he'd been proven right on both fronts. The swelling had thankfully subsided and being in close proximity to a bed had indeed been most convenient.

The downside of such a plan, however, was that at some point during one such lust-filled occasion her laptop must have got in the way because when she returned to it half an hour later—still breathless, still dizzy—she found that the operating system had somehow disappeared.

'I'm seriously impressed,' she said, lying back against a pile of pillows and watching as, beside her, a naked-from-the-waist-up Santi applied his programming magic to the device.

'By this? Compared to some of the things I've worked on, this is child's play.'

For a moment, she admired the way his long, tanned fingers flew over the keyboard and thought, with a delicious shiver, of the way they'd skimmed over her. 'What's been the most complicated?'

'The global online payment system was a challenge,' he said as pages of incomprehensible data started flashing up on the black screen. 'It took years to develop. Coding isn't always logic and predictability. One tiny glitch can bring the whole thing crashing down. Luckily we were able to identify the bugs and iron them out before going live but it was extremely stressful for months.'

She knew all about stress. Although he was doing a pretty good job of relieving some of hers, he still clammed up whenever she tried to talk to him about anything in his past. He was monosyllabic on pretty much any topic other than sex and work and it was becoming increasingly frustrating. So much for his wanting to make things up to her. And so much for turning his brain to soup.

Perhaps it would do them good to get away for a bit, she mused while he continued to fiddle with her laptop—out of this room, out of the house and leave all this behind for a while. Perhaps getting out and into nature was the way to find out more about the man she was sleeping with. She hadn't been the only one to let her guard down the afternoon they'd gone whale watching, and she wanted to see more of the country that he clearly loved so much, beyond these four walls and views of the south Atlantic.

'How far away are the Iguazu Falls?' she asked as he hit a button that to her relief turned the screen back to an interface she recognised.

'A couple of hours by plane. Why?'

'I've heard they're spectacular. One of the seven wonders of the natural world, I read.'

'They are.'

'I'd like to see them. Will you take me?'

He slid her a glance, his expression oddly unreadable. 'When?'

'No time like the present.'

'I'm not a tour guide,' he said with a slow shake of his head, 'and you have a sprained ankle.'

That? Pah.

'It's had plenty of rest. It's as good as new.'

'We're here to work.'

'I'll stay an extra day in lieu.'

'No.'

'Please?'

'Borrow my plane and go on your own when we're done.'

What would be the point of that? 'I feel we could do with a break,' she said, more than happy to use his own arguments against him while her laptop's operating system steadily updated. 'We've barely left this room in thirty-six hours. We could do with fresh air and a different view. I went whale watching and survived.'

'That was one afternoon.'

'It's still early. We could be back by this evening. And just think of all that nature you like so much. All that untamed wildness. I imagine there's no place like it on earth.'

'There isn't.'

'When were you last there?'

'Two years ago.' The look he gave her was pointed. 'But if you're about to tell me it's time for a revisit you'll be wasting your breath.'

Desperate times called for desperate measures, and she had every intention of getting what she wanted, so she fluttered her eyelids and lowered her voice. 'I'll make it worth your while.'

He stilled. A flicker of heat flared in the depths of his eyes and a thrilling little wave of satisfaction rippled through her. 'How?'

She leaned over and whispered in his ear, taking care not to dislodge her laptop, most gratified to hear his breathing shallow and to feel his jaw clench as she explained in great detail exactly how she'd be expressing her appreciation.

'Fine,' he muttered when she'd finished, thrusting the device at her—which now showed the familiar login box, the clever man—and flinging back the sheets. 'Pack a change of clothes and your passport. I'll alert the crew.'

* * *

Santi didn't want to analyse how swiftly he'd caved into Thalia's demands—or why. However much she might intimate that he still owed her for what he'd said in Paris, accommodating her wishes wasn't what was required here. But then she'd whispered those sweet nothings into his ear and he'd surrendered in a heartbeat, justifying the move by telling himself that she clearly wasn't going to let it go and he'd run out of excuses anyway.

But there was still the opportunity to snatch victory from the jaws of defeat, he thought darkly as they pulled up at the airport twenty minutes after they'd left the house. He'd made a whole raft of arrangements that meant he could hang out in a nearby hotel and leave her to it for the day. He'd already viewed the falls from a multitude of angles and taken a boat up the river. He could still vividly recall the fascinating hike through the forest and the swim beneath a waterfall that had come at the end of it. He didn't need to do any of that again and she didn't need a chaperone.

What he *did* need was to prevent any further attempts she made at profound conversation by getting her to make good on her promises. So the minute they boarded his plane he took her hand and chivvied her down the aisle to the cabin at the rear.

'Are you planning on calling in my debt now?' she said, a little breathless as he pushed open the door and ushered her in.

'Is that a problem?'

'No. But it's a good thing it's not a zero-sum game.'

He closed the door and flipped the lock. 'Every-one's a winner.'

'I had very distracting thoughts the last time we were in here.'

'Show me.'

Dark eyes gleaming with heat and excitement, Thalia planted one hand on his chest and pushed. He fell back onto the bed and she straddled him, her hands making swift work of his belt and fly. Heart thundering, desire throbbing in every cell of his being, he lifted his hips and she shifted to pull down his trousers and shorts. Then she wrapped her hand around his achingly hard length and dipped her head. He closed his eyes and gave himself up to sensation.

When she took him in her mouth he groaned and shook. Within moments, he was tangling his fingers in her hair, muttering incoherent words in Portuguese even he didn't understand. She upped the pressure and he shuddered, the exquisite tension building, and he was soon so close he could feel the familiar waves of pleasure surging, so close he was losing the ability to think, and so when she stopped, abruptly lifting her-self off him and taking her velvety wet warmth with her, he could have wept.

He opened his eyes, prepared to beg if he had to, but a second later she was back, naked from the waist down. She deftly rolled on protection—he gritted his teeth so hard they nearly shattered—and then with his assistance and a thick hoarse moan sank down onto him.

His head spun. His pulse pounded. She leaned forwards, sealing her mouth to his in a crushing kiss, moved—once, twice, a third time—and then she was shaking and juddering and panting so wildly it tipped him over the edge. Gripping her hips, he thrust up hard and exploded, pulsating into her so powerfully and for so long it hollowed him out.

'That was something else,' he said, once he'd caught his breath and his head had stopped spinning.

'I promised you membership of the mile-high club,' she said with a blinding smile that whipped the air from his lungs and made his chest contract. 'And I always keep my promises.'

So did he, he thought as he rolled her onto her back. And buried his face in her neck so he could not get caught up in the wicked merriment dancing in her eyes and lose what was left of his mind. Especially those promises he made to himself.

Rendered dazed and weak-limbed by their antics in the cabin, which had only got wilder with the soaring altitude, Thalia briefly considered it a shame they had to land. But her disappointment vanished the instant they transferred to the helicopter that Santi had arranged to ferry them to their destination. They took off, veered to the right, and almost instantly they were flying over the thick dark green forest of the vast national park, which stretched out to the horizon as far as the eye could see in all directions. In the distance, a cloud of spray rose up over the trees into the azure sky. A sliver of river came into view and grew into a wide murky brown ribbon that cut a winding swathe through the flat landscape.

With every passing moment, the anticipation rushing through her swelled. This approach allowed for a build-up, which was almost unbearable. And then there were the falls, down on her right, at the point where the river curved into the shape of a horseshoe— hundreds of cataracts of varying heights and widths, a roaring, tumbling force of nature, so awe-inspiring and magnificent that she found she was pressing her nose up against the glass, her breath catching in her throat.

'This is the largest waterfall system in the world,' Santi shouted, leaning in close so she could hear him over the whirring of the helicopter's blades, the buffeting wind and the extraordinary thunder of water below. 'It's nearly three kilometres wide. There are two hundred and seventy-five individual falls that drop eighty metres into the river below. Only twenty percent are on this side. The rest are in Argentina. The border runs right through the middle of the Garganta del Diablo.'

'What's that?'

'The Devil's Throat. That one there.'

Leaning around her, he pointed to the largest fall, down which water crashed powerfully into a creamy white pool. It was almost indistinguishable, thanks to the mist it must have been generating for millions of years.

'Can we get any closer?'

'On foot and by boat you can. See that walkway? It takes you right on top of it.'

'Will we be doing that?'

'If you'd like.'

She flashed him a grin. 'I truly cannot wait.'

The helicopter landed a short time later on the helipad at the Hotel das Cataratas, where they grabbed a quick sandwich and, in response to her stream of questions about the local area, Santi revealed an extensive knowledge of the local flora and fauna.

'Because of the spray, the micro-climate of the rainforest here is subtropical,' he said, resting his elbows on the railing of the terrace beyond which the waterfalls roared and coated them in droplets. 'It's home to all sorts of wildlife.'

'Such as?'

'Tapirs, giant anteaters, howler monkeys, ocelots, caimans. The last time I was here, I spotted a jaguar. That was a moment. If you're lucky you'll see some of them this afternoon. I've ordered a car to take you across the border into Argentina. From there you can cross the walkway above the falls and hike through the forest. There are many trails to choose from. None of them is particularly challenging.'

Thalia stared out at the view, not caring about getting drenched, only thinking she could listen to him for hours. The passion in his voice... The depth of his knowledge... But then his words registered and she turned to him, frowning. 'Are you not coming with me?'

'I wasn't planning on it,' he said with a quick apologetic smile. 'Thanks to you, I have work to do.'

'Oh.' Her shoulders dropped. Her stomach plummeted. That was disappointing. And not because she wouldn't be able to quiz him further and learn more about him. She was enjoying his company. She'd never had it quite like this before, and she wanted more. 'That's a shame. I was looking forward to an insider's guide. Your expertise. What if I get lost? What if I fall in?'

'You won't.'

'It won't be the same without you.'

He studied her for a moment, a faint frown creasing his brow as if he were battling with himself, then he gave a shrug and said, 'I guess work can wait.'

CHAPTER ELEVEN

THALIA COULD NOT have been more delighted that Santi had shelved his plans to accommodate hers. She could easily have gone alone and hired a guide of her own if she'd felt the need, but if she'd had, she'd have missed out on the tales he'd told her of his travels around the country. She wouldn't have learned about the wildlife of the Pantanal, the boat trip he'd once taken down a piranha-infested tributary of the Amazon, or riding a beach buggy among the dunes of the northeast coast, one of the last places left on the planet with hundreds of miles of unobstructed sand.

She would never forget the thrill of standing above the falls, hearing and feeling the powerful rush of cascading water beneath her feet. The sheer jaw-dropping magnificence of the sight had blown her mind and yet she hadn't been able to keep from sliding glances in Santi's direction. She hadn't been able to stop thinking that he was pretty jaw-dropping and magnificent too.

After returning to the riverbank, they trekked along a trail that led deep into the forest. He pointed out an ocelot and she spied an eagle. Being so far off the beaten track, they didn't come across any other visitors.

So when they arrived at a set of stairs that descended into a wooded area they didn't think twice about stripping off and diving into the large deep crystal-clear pool into which poured more frothing water.

'I don't think I've ever seen anything so staggeringly beautiful,' said Thalia, floating lazily on her back and gazing up at the sky and around her at the forested sides of the pool.

'Neither have I,' muttered Santi as he pulled her squealing with shock and delight into his arms and shut her up with his mouth and his hands, at which point she thought there might be something of her exhibitionist mother in her after all.

By the time they returned from the boat trip that had given her another equally exciting experience—although at that point she'd run out of superlatives to describe what she saw and how she felt about it—it was too late to go anywhere else, so he booked them into a suite at the hotel and ordered dinner to be sent up to the room.

'Thank you for today,' she said over coffee, feeling replete, molten-hearted and completely overwhelmed by everything she'd seen and heard. 'It's been amazing. I can't remember the last time anyone other than a paid employee organised anything for me. I've spent a decade devoting my time to helping others. It's been lovely to be on the receiving end of such attention for a change, even if I did coerce you into it.'

'You're welcome.'

'Your knowledge of the area is seriously impressive.'

'As I may have mentioned once or twice, I like

nature.' He swung his gaze from the view to hers, a smile hovering at his mouth, and she couldn't help swooning a little. 'It's not just that I grew up with very little of it. It's also that while it can be organised, systematic and comprehensive, unlike coding, it's not at all logical.'

'Isn't it?' She had no clue. She was just enjoying the way his mouth moved.

'Logic is a human intellectual construction,' he said as he lifted his coffee cup to his lips. 'Nature is the opposite of that. I find the dichotomy fascinating.'

She found *him* fascinating, she thought dreamily. He was tough and dominant yet could also be caring and thoughtful, even when it went against his better judgement. If she wasn't careful, she could be in danger of becoming smitten all over again. 'Why on earth have you never married?'

It was unfortunate that at that moment he'd taken a mouthful of coffee because it clearly went down the wrong way. He coughed. He spluttered. He put the cup down with a clatter and gave his chest a thump. 'That's a very personal question,' he said a little hoarsely as he dabbed his eyes with a napkin.

It was. No doubt about it. But she'd been pussyfooting around topics that were personal to him for long enough and now she wanted answers. 'You're thirty-four and highly eligible. It's curious.'

'It's also none of your business.'

That was true too, but that didn't mean she had any intention of giving up. 'Have you never met anyone special?'

'We're not discussing this.'

Oh, yes, they were. 'Do you have a problem with commitment?'

A flare of heat flickered in the dark depths of his eyes, as if he truly believed he could detract her that way. 'Whatever happened to just sex?'

'To echo what you once said, we have to talk about something.'

'No, we don't. If you're finished here we can go back to bed where I'll show you how very much we do not have to talk about anything.'

Thalia ignored the wave of desire that spread through her at that darkly delivered promise, and focused. 'Do you mind not having anyone to share your success with?'

Evidently realising she had no intention of quitting this conversation, Santi gave a deep sigh of what was clearly exasperation and said, 'No.'

'Don't you get lonely?'

'No.'

'Lucky you. I do.'

'Then sort out your issues with your brother.'

Thalia frowned. That wasn't what she'd meant, but she was hardly going to confess to him that the source of her loneliness was a lack of romance caused by her many hangups, so she went with his interpretation. 'It's not that easy.'

'It might be. For all you know he might be finding things as difficult as you are.'

'That's highly doubtful,' she said, trying not to sound morose but failing. 'He has other things to keep him occupied, like a wife, and in six months' time a baby. Zoe's pregnant.'

'Oh? I must send her my congratulations.'

'There'll be even less time for me once he or she arrives.'

'You might find the opposite thing happens and your relationship gets stronger.'

She stared at him, the majestic backdrop of the falls momentarily forgotten, the previous dreaminess history. 'How on earth do you figure that?'

'You'll have to cram more into less time. That would be pretty intense, I imagine.'

'You're mad.'

'I might be right. Have you ever considered that it can't be easy for Zoe either, having to share Atticus with you?'

No, she hadn't, but that wasn't the point. 'What would you know about it?'

'Not a lot, I admit.'

'Well, then.'

'I'm just thinking logically.'

Thalia bristled. 'Are you implying that I'm not?'

'You could be being blinded by emotion.'

'Blinded by emotion?' she echoed in indignation.

'I get that the apple cart's been upset,' he said while she wondered if he was even aware of the dangerous path he was treading. 'But you have had months to deal with it.'

The *apple cart*? It was an entire bloody orchard that had been uprooted. 'I'm aware of that.'

'Has it occurred to you that you might be squandering a perfectly good sibling out of obstinacy?'

What? For a moment, she had no words. Did he think she wanted to be this conflicted? That she didn't want to find a way through the mess she'd been in for close to two years? 'That is *not* what I'm doing.'

'Then why don't you just talk to him?'

He had no idea. It wasn't that simple. How could she explain to Atticus how she felt? What would she say? Would he even listen? And what if she somehow ended up losing him for good? After all, he did have someone else to share his life with now. Soon he'd have two someone-elses, and probably more in the future. He didn't need her. He might never have needed her. It was all just so hard, like stumbling around on uncharted territory at night without a torch or a compass, and by suggesting it was her fault she was in this mess Santi wasn't helping. 'You don't have siblings so I don't expect you to understand.'

He tensed. Frowned as if lost in thought for a moment. Then gave a shrug. 'My mistake.'

Much later, while Thalia slumbered beside him in the moonlight, Santi stared up at the ceiling of the hotel room, his head pounding, his stomach roiling, and thought that that was just one of many mistakes he'd made today.

The first was agreeing to bring her here when there'd been absolutely no reason to. The second was throwing aside his plans to leave her to explore the waterfalls on her own and accompanying her around the site instead. The latest was bringing the topic of her brother up over coffee in the first place.

He should never have done that. He should never have allowed the simmering envy and resentment he'd suddenly felt to get the better of him. He'd been so close to confessing that she was wrong and he *did* have a sibling that he could scarcely believe it.

Why on earth would he want to *do* that? It made no sense at all. If he hadn't stopped himself at the last minute, biting back the words piling up in his head, he'd have had to admit that he'd never met his half-sister, despite knowing perfectly well who she was. At which point Thalia would have probably—and rightly—called him a hypocrite and accused him of very much not practising what he preached. Following that, no doubt, she'd have continued to prod around his psyche until she'd uncovered all his secrets, all his complexes, and he could never allow that.

He'd been unsettled by the day, that was the trouble. He'd assumed that he'd have everything under control, but once again he could not have been more wrong. The minute he'd glimpsed Thalia's disappointment when he'd told her to go it alone, the promise he'd made to himself to keep emotion out of what they were doing vaporised. He hadn't liked the disappearance of her smile or the dimming of her enthusiasm. He'd liked even less knowing that he was the one who'd crushed both. He'd compensated by deciding to show her everything and then oversharing his fascination with nature, so captivated by her engagement with what he was saying he'd overshared some more.

And then, as if that hadn't been worrying enough, she'd started firing questions at him over coffee about marriage and commitment and loneliness. He didn't generally dwell much on such things. He was fine with his life as it was. He never analysed the decisions he made when it came to relationships, until he'd had one with her, which had ended, at which point he'd then seemed to do nothing but. Why was she even interested in such things? She'd better not have changed her mind about the purely carnal nature of what they were doing.

Whatever had been behind that conversation, she had the potential to be as dangerous as he'd feared. She battered his defences and threatened his inhibitions and had him abandoning the promises he'd made to himself left right and centre. He enjoyed spending time with her way too much, and if he wasn't extremely careful he might well find himself spilling his guts to her and questioning every value he lived by, and that simply could not happen. He would not give her that power. He would never be in her thrall again.

He didn't want to contemplate what might have happened if they hadn't split up last August. Or how long it had taken him to get over her. And he definitely didn't want to think about why he'd really lashed out in Paris, which he suspected deep down had had nothing to do with hurt pride and a dent in his track record and everything to do with his bone-deep fear of rejection. All that was going on here was work and sex for another four days—back at the house to which they'd be heading first thing in the morning and from which they would not move again—and that was the way it would stay.

CHAPTER TWELVE

WHEN THALIA'S FRIEND in Rio messaged her at ten on Sunday morning to invite her to lunch later that day, she had no hesitation in saying yes. Her irritation with Santi for providing an unsolicited, uninformed opinion on her relationship with her brother hadn't dampened her desire for him one iota—if anything, tinged with a certain edginess, the sex had been even hotter—but instead of lessening since they'd returned from Iguazu at the crack of dawn yesterday, her frustration had intensified.

She did not appreciate the implication that she was being immature and petulant. Alone in the world for the last fifteen years, he knew absolutely nothing about anything when it came to family. Or her. If he did, he'd know that obstinacy was not behind her reluctance to speak to her brother. Fear was. She feared rejection, she'd forced herself to acknowledge, because—annoyingly—she had found herself mulling over his observation and wondering if it had some merit. She feared discovering that everything she'd believed to be true about their relationship was a lie and that her entire life was built on sand. That was why she hadn't called him in months and kept the conversations short when he rang her. Ignorance and denial were way more appealing than the truth and potential devastation.

Nevertheless, part of her wished she hadn't pushed the conversation into such sensitive territory the night before last. She hadn't learned anything new about Santi and the lovely day they'd spent together was now stained with sourness. Breakfast on the hotel terrace had been an exercise in excruciating politeness, the tension as thick and cold as the tropical fruit smoothies they'd been served, and the atmosphere since then had only become more strained.

She didn't know how to fix it. Or quite what there was to fix. All she did know was that she could do with some time and space away from him to regain perspective and regroup. The last week had been a huge upheaval and insanely intense, and lately the pressure had been compounded by a severe lack of sleep.

So, with the details of lunch arranged, she made a call to her family's personal private office in Athens and then abruptly closed her laptop.

'I'm going to the city,' she announced, gathering up her things up from the table and getting to her feet.

Santi whipped his head round, his dark simmering gaze colliding with hers, and she had to steel herself not to respond to the inevitable wave of heat that swept through her. 'I'm sorry?'

'I'm meeting that friend of mine in Rio for lunch. She lives in Ipanema. I haven't seen her for years. It'll be good to catch up. And don't worry, I'm not playing hooky. She's on the board of a number of South America based charities. She'd be an excellent addition to yours. I can't imagine she'll take much persuading. She's like me—has had a lot, keen to pay it back.'

He sat back, all broad strong shoulders and loose powerful limbs, and frowned. 'Ipanema is a three-hour drive.'

'Which is why I've ordered a helicopter. I noticed the day I arrived here that you had a helipad,' she said in response to the sharp raise of his eyebrows, 'and as you once pointed out I have resources. It'll be here in half an hour.'

'That's quick.'

'My family are very good customers.'

'When will you be back?'

'I'm not sure. I may stay overnight. Don't wait up.'

Santi was now beginning to look at her as though she'd slapped him round the face with a wet fish, but he'd get over it. He might even find the time apart useful. Perhaps he could sort out whatever was on his mind that had him scowling about the place. She understood that she'd fired some uncomfortable questions at him in Iguazu but they hadn't been that bad. It wasn't as if she'd asked him for commitment or anything. She'd merely been curious. So if that *was* why he was being all chilly and aloof—rather an overreaction, she felt—then no doubt he'd welcome some space as much as she did.

But in all honesty, she didn't much care what he was thinking right now. She just wanted to escape, catch up with her friend and stop feeling so conflicted about everything for a while.

'Have a great day,' she said, and, with the tight flash of a smile, left.

The trip to Rio turned out to be exactly what Thalia needed, although far more surprising than she could ever have anticipated.

The minute the helicopter rose into the air the weight lifted from her chest and she felt as though she could breathe for the first time in days. The tension gripping her muscles melted clean away. The bubbling desire and sensory overload that were ever present when she was in Santi's vicinity vanished. She hadn't realised she'd been in such danger of once again becoming wholly encompassed by him. What they were doing would come to an end on Wednesday, and the opportunity to reset could not have come at a better time.

The route east took her over the sparkling sea of the south Atlantic. Below, on her left, tree-covered hills became villages that grew into suburbs that turned into the sprawl of city itself, built around the beautiful Guanabara Bay and overlooked by the iconic statue of Cristo Redentor.

On landing, she took a taxi from the heliport through the streets of the city to the beach bar in Ipanema. She found her friend sitting at a table on the sand with a pair of caipirinhas in front of her and Sugarloaf Mountain behind.

She'd met Gaby, an internationally renowned su-

permodel from Copacabana, five years ago at a fundraiser in Marrakech, which she'd organised in aid of
cancer research. They'd been introduced, had immediately hit it off and had stayed in touch. She hadn't
seen her for a couple of years now, but as Thalia embraced her friend and sat down, somehow it felt like
yesterday.

'I can't believe you're working and staying with
Santiago Ferreira,' said Gaby, still clearly gobsmacked
by the revelation one hour, a lot of conversation and a
large platter of seafood later.

Thalia broke off a chunk of soft cheese bread and
dipped it into a bowl of fragrant aioli. 'I can't quite
believe it myself.'

'What's he like?'

Ruthless, aggravating, sexy as hell. 'Impressive,'
she said, knowing Gaby well but not quite well enough
to go into explicit detail. 'Very good at getting what
he wants and beyond handsome in an untamed kind
of a way.'

'Nice?'

Nice was far too anodyne a word for a man like
him, but he'd fed her well, shown her some incredible sites and taken good care of her ankle, so when
he wasn't being domineering or moody or challenging
or single-mindedly giving her more pleasure than she
thought she could bear, she supposed he was rather
nice. 'I take it you haven't met him.'

'I haven't, but I very much want to.'

'Oh?' Thalia glanced over at her lovely, stunning
friend with her short white blonde hair, her willowy

height and perfect figure. The shaft of jealousy that whipped the air from her lungs caught her by surprise. 'Why?'

'Because he looks exactly like my father.'

The jealousy evaporated. Her eyebrows shot up. She nearly choked on the piece of bread she'd just put into her mouth. 'Seriously?'

'The resemblance is uncanny,' said Gaby, taking a sip of her soda water. 'They share the same features. Eyes, nose, mouth. Even the cowlick. When he hit the news with that deal it was such a fascinating rag to riches tale that the press couldn't get enough of him. His photo started popping up everywhere.'

'I know.' She'd been doing a pretty good job of forgetting all about him until then.

'I was on a lilo the first time I saw one. It was such a shock I nearly fell into the pool.'

'He can have that effect on people,' said Thalia, thinking with a shiver of her own unplanned midnight dip the other night. 'So what are you saying? Do you think your father could also be his?'

'It's possible,' said Gaby with a faint shrug. 'I read that he didn't know who his was and mine wasn't the nicest of men. He had multiple affairs. That was why my mother eventually divorced him. I do hope he is. Or if not a half-brother, a cousin or something. I'm disappointingly devoid of relatives.'

'What does your mother say about it?'

'She's as in the dark as I am, but she did remark that nothing would surprise her when it comes to my father.'

Well. This was an intriguing turn of events. If by some chance, Gaby's father was also Santi's—and now she was looking, she could see that her friend and Santi shared a jawline, which was quite possibly why she'd felt as though she'd last seen Gaby way more recently than two years ago—then it meant that he wasn't all alone on this planet, after all. And that was such a relief because no one should be, in her opinion. Her family regularly bewildered, confused and distressed her in different ways—especially over the last year or so—but she couldn't imagine life without them. Deep down, she could now admit, it had been bothering her that Santi had no one.

'What are your plans for the rest of the day?' she said, the seed of a plan taking root in her head even while the excitement drumming through her drowned out the voice of her conscience that warned her not to interfere—that it wasn't her place to manage anything, especially a potential bombshell like this, that this wasn't the way to fix the simmering awkwardness, and, above all, she could not make up for the strained relations between her and her brother by fixing those between Gaby and hers.

'Not a lot. I'm between jobs. Why?'

'Why don't you come back with me this evening and meet him?'

'Are you sure that would be wise?'

'Of course,' she said, so determined to make it happen that nothing else mattered. 'Not only has he acquired an experienced and enthusiastic trustee, but he might also have gained a sister. A great one. Who wouldn't be thrilled by that?'

'Maybe we should call ahead first.'

'And spoil the surprise?'

'All right,' said Gaby with a flash of the megawatt grin that had made her famous. 'Let's do it.'

Once he'd got over his shock at Thalia's abrupt departure, Santi had initially been delighted at the prospect of her lunch in the city. Her off his property and out of his hair was exactly what he'd been after before she'd tripped and sprained her ankle and scuppered the idea of either putting her on his plane or getting on it himself.

Things between them had been frosty since they'd returned from Iguazu. He hadn't been able to shake the feeling that he was hurtling along a perilous road that he couldn't get off, and worse, possibly didn't even *want* to get off.

He told himself that without her distracting presence he could work on obliterating the thoughts of his father and half-sister, which kept bothering him with irritating persistence. He could knuckle down to completing the tasks she'd set him, with which he hadn't yet got very far. He could catch up on some much-needed sleep.

But to his immense frustration, none of that happened. Disappointingly, once again, out of sight was not out of mind, and his concentration remained shot. The scent of her lingered in his bed, rendering sleep impossible. He prowled round the house, trying and failing to find something to take his mind off the fact that she wasn't there, and achieving nothing.

He kept wondering where she was, what she was doing and whether she was all right. Rio could be dangerous for the uninitiated. Regardless of the tense state of affairs, he should have insisted on going with her, even though the city held few good memories and he avoided it where possible. He lost count of the number of times he grabbed his phone to call her before tossing it away in disgust.

When she walked through the door, just after six, the relief that spun through him nearly took out his knees. She'd obviously decided against staying overnight. Because she couldn't wait to get back to him? He could not afford to let his thoughts head in that direction. So instead, with effort, he contemplated the bemusing absence of whirring helicopter blades sounds—she must have driven back—and strode into the hall to greet her.

The plan was to apologise profusely for his recent moodiness—it wasn't her fault his past was trying to muscle in on his present—and then throw her over his shoulder and cart her off to bed. But she wasn't alone, and when he saw who she was with he slammed to a sudden halt, the breath whipping from his lungs, the floor tilting violently beneath his feet, his head draining of every thought he'd ever had.

'Santi,' Thalia said with a breezy smile, as if she wasn't blasting apart his carefully constructed lie of thirty-four years and shattering his entire existence by bringing this woman here. 'This is my friend, Gabriela Cardoso.'

A cold sweat broke out all over his skin. His stomach churned. He knew who she was. He'd seen her face staring out of countless billboards, magazines, newspapers. It had haunted his dreams more often than he liked to admit. He'd never expected to see it right in front of him. Could he even begin to hope that her being here, with Thalia, in his house, was nothing more than some kind of horrific coincidence?

'Prazer em te conocer,' he said thickly as he held out his hand for Gabriela to shake, even though he wasn't pleased to meet her at all. He was, in fact, shocked and petrified—as he'd always been. Because what if the truth came out about their shared parentage and she too slammed a metaphorical door in his face?

His pulse hammering, his head pounding, he wrenched his gaze from his half-sister and turned it on Thalia. 'What's this all about?'

'Firstly, she's agreed to be on the board of your charity and, secondly, she suspects you might be related. Isn't that great?'

Thalia was beaming, as if delighted with her cleverness in bringing this about, but there was no 'might' and nothing 'great' about any of it. He was burning up. He felt light-headed. He was going to vomit. Pass out. Quite possibly both.

'You had no right.'

Her smile vanished and she frowned. 'What?'

He couldn't handle this. He was totally unprepared. Emotion was surging through him in great rolling waves and his control was unravelling so fast that it was going to be history within seconds.

'Excuse me,' he said, backing away as if both women were brandishing weapons at him, which, in a way, they were. 'I have some calls to make.'

Well, that was not the reaction she'd been expecting, thought Thalia, eyes wide, jaw on the floor as Santi spun on his heel and stalked off as if being chased by a prowl of hungry jaguars.

If she'd allowed herself to give it much thought, which stupidly—she now realised—she hadn't, she'd would have said she'd anticipated surprise, yes, but also joy, a tear and a hug or two, and perhaps even a little gratitude. She would never have expected thunderclouds and retreat, even though things between them lately had been fraught. So what on earth was going on?

'I think we can safely say he's not overjoyed to meet me,' came the dry observation from her right. 'I told you we should have called.'

She turned to Gaby, swallowing hard. 'I'm so sorry,' she said, mortified and appalled in equal measure. 'I had no idea he was going to do that. He must have gone into shock.'

'I suspect it's more than that,' said her friend, her expression thoughtful, though she had paled a little. 'Did you see the look on his face when he first laid eyes on me? It was as if he'd seen a ghost. He knew who I was before you suggested it.'

Thalia frowned. Santi had never known who his father was, so how could he know about Gaby? It didn't make sense. 'That's impossible.'

'It's unlikely, I admit, but it's not impossible.'

'But that would mean he's been lying to the world. And why would he deny knowing you?'

'You'd have to ask him.'

'I don't think I dare,' she said with a wince. 'I don't think I've ever seen anyone quite so angry.'

'Look, I'm going to head off,' said Gaby, hitching her bag higher on her shoulder and turning to walk out the way she'd just come in. 'It's a long drive back to the city.'

Thalia followed her out to her car, every step she took as heavy as a lead weight. 'I'm really sorry,' she said, her voice tight and small. 'This is all my doing. I feel terrible.'

'Don't worry about. Really. I'm glad to have met him, even if it was for a nanosecond. It's a start. I hope. Give him my number and tell him he can call me any time if he wants to. Let me know about the trusteeship. I'd be really interested in it but not if it's going to be difficult. Good luck.'

Thalia waved her friend off, her head spinning, her entire body trembling. Somehow, without intending to, she'd messed up badly. She'd presumed. She'd overstepped. She'd been arrogant and unthinking and not just with regards to Santi. Despite Gaby's reassurances, her friend *wasn't* all right with what had happened. She'd caught the searing disappointment that had flashed across her face, and it piled guilt onto the remorse. She did not deserve to be let off as lightly as she had been. She'd call her tomorrow to check she'd got home safely and find out how she genuinely was about this. But in the meantime, she had to track Santi down. She owed him an apology too.

She found him sitting on the terrace necking a bottle of rum and she paused for a second, her heart hammering and her breath short. She felt a bit sick, thanks to the regret knotting her stomach, but she could not run off to the hotel that was currently closed for business and she could not leave things this way. She stepped forward and cleared her throat, preparing to apologise, grovel if she had to, but he got in first.

'How dare you ambush me like that in my own home?'

She flinched at the quiet cold fury she could hear in his voice and swallowed down the hot lump in her throat. 'I'm so sorry,' she said, rubbing her hands down her trousers as she came to a stop in front of him. 'It was never my intention to cause you distress. I thought you'd be pleased.'

His expression was darker and harder than she'd ever seen it and her chest tightened. 'Whatever gave you that idea?'

'I don't know.' She shook her head, unable to work out quite what she'd been thinking at the time. 'When Gaby told me that she suspected her father could be yours, I just got overexcited by the thought of you finding out you had a long-lost half-sister. I might have been projecting my issues with my brother onto you and her. But I was way out of line. It's none of my business.'

'Precisely.'

'I should never have interfered.'

'No. You shouldn't.'

'I should have given you her number and let you deal with it in your own way.'

'You should.'

She bit her lip, desperate to make up for her mistakes. 'But if there was anything you wanted to talk about, I'm very good at listening.'

The silence that fell then was deafening. He appeared to be utterly speechless. He just glared at her, incredulity written all over his darkly handsome face, before he eventually snapped, 'Are you joking?'

'You might find sharing whatever it is you're thinking cathartic.'

'You have no idea what you've done.'

Her cheeks burned. Her eyes stung. 'Tell me so I can fix it.'

'Leave me alone.'

CHAPTER THIRTEEN

AT THE BOTTOM of the bottle, Santi had to admit defeat. He had hoped that copious quantities of rum would obliterate the emotions that had broken free of their bonds and were now rampaging through him, but they hadn't. He was stone-cold sober, still in turmoil, still unable to get a grip on anything. The past and the present had collided, the resulting compound had imploded, and all the old feelings he thought he'd successfully buried—the rejection, the bewilderment, the anger and resentment—were thundering through him like a tornado.

And all because Thalia had gone for lunch.

His head was pounding. His pulse was racing and the air pressure seemed to have dropped. He was finding it hard to breathe. How was he to find peace? That was the question ricocheting around his brain as he rubbed his chest and forced some warm evening air into his lungs before he passed out. Shoving everything back in the box from which it had escaped felt like a Sisyphean task. Rum clearly wasn't the answer. Nor was gazing up and out into the dark starry sky, which had always filled him with a sense of serenity, but tonight was having no effect on him at all.

Perhaps the solution, then, was escape. There was nothing keeping him here. Thalia's ankle was fine. He could leave right this minute, put as much distance between himself and the two women who were causing him the kind of torment he hadn't been subjected to for years. Then he could throw himself into mentoring budding entrepreneurs in a place far, far away.

But would that actually solve anything?

Wouldn't the maelstrom follow him wherever he went?

Contrary to what he'd always assumed, he evidently hadn't dealt with the past. He hadn't buried anything. It had all just lurked in the recesses of his mind until Thalia had blithely come along and shone a spotlight on it, turning his entire world to chaos.

Maybe he should seek professional help instead. He'd never really considered it before, but that was how other people seemed to vanquish their demons. The thought of discussing his with Thalia, as she'd suggested, made him want to throw up. The exposure... The vulnerability... The surrender of power... Just imagining it raised the hairs at the back of his neck and covered his skin in goosebumps. And how could she help anyway? Just because she'd spent months of working through her own issues with family didn't mean she'd be any good at unravelling his. Their situations were entirely different.

Although, were they?

Both stemmed from the sort of dysfunction that

should have led to state involvement but, for very different reasons, hadn't. Both aroused emotions of the negative kind—jealousy and resentment in her, anger and bitterness in him. Both had lain dormant until an external force had made them erupt.

So might she understand the feelings he was experiencing and the causes of them? Might she have some insight into how to handle them? He certainly wasn't making much progress on his own, and it was her fault he was in this mess. She'd stirred the hornet's nest, so maybe he *should* task her with fixing it. Quite frankly, however tough it might be to open up to her, things couldn't get much worse.

Before he could think better of it, Santi slammed the bottle down and surged to his feet. He strode to her room, knocked once on the door, and then, without waiting for an answer, barged in.

'What are you doing?' he said, coming to an abrupt halt, his brows snapping together in a deep frown at the sight of her clothes strewn all over the bed.

'Packing. I'll go in the morning.'

Well, *that* wasn't happening. Not now he'd decided to seek her advice. Not at all, in fact. 'No. Stop. I want to talk to you. About Gabriela.'

She stilled. Her gaze flew to his. 'Oh. No. Really. You don't have to do that.'

'You were the one who suggested it,' he said, stalking to the chair in the corner and throwing himself into it. 'You said you could fix this and you owe me.'

Looking pale and contrite, Thalia swallowed hard and gave a nod. 'All right,' she said, putting down the pair of trousers she'd been folding and sinking down onto the edge of the bed. 'I'll do my best.'

With a shove of his hands through his hair and a clench of his jaw, Santi braced himself and ground out, 'Her father *is* my father and she *is* my half-sister.'

'How long have you known?'

'About him, ever since I can remember,' he said, fighting to keep his heartrate down and his breathing even. 'He met my mother in the bar where she used to sing in the evenings. They had an affair that resulted in me. He wanted her to terminate the pregnancy. She didn't.'

Eyes widening, Thalia emitted a tiny gasp. 'That's awful.'

Yes, well, it didn't stop there. 'He was an extremely successful businessman,' he went on gruffly. 'She tried to get financial support out of him but he maintained that it was her choice to have me and refused. He strung her along for another decade before discarding her. He'd married a debutante. My mother was nothing more than his bit of rough.'

Thalia winced and he wished he could have put it a different way, but the truth could be ugly. 'And he never met you?'

'Not once.'

Her expression hardened, as if she was outraged on his behalf, which he found oddly comforting. 'What a bastard. I'm not surprised you've always claimed not to know anything about him.'

'It was just easier to pretend he never existed.'

'I completely get that. The situation sounds beyond painful. You must have been so angry and hurt.'

'I was,' he agreed, marvelling at her ability to get straight to the heart of it. 'Living where I did didn't help. There were many outlets for that anger, none of them good. When I was fourteen, one of my friends was killed in fight over gang territory. I wanted vengeance so badly it burned me up inside and it would have been very easy to get it. But in the nick of time I was scooped up by a charity who worked in the neighbourhood. They gave me a mentor who showed me another way out.'

She tilted her head. 'Coding?'

'Right,' he confirmed with a nod. 'Aside from challenging my brain, it calmed me down and gave me the space and peace to think. I realised that getting a grip on the anger and all the other emotions I was struggling to deal with was simply a question of control. There was so much I couldn't do anything about. My response to it all, I could. It became a way of life.' Until he'd met her, at which point that life had gone to hell in a handcart.

'That makes sense. So when did you find out about Gaby?'

'I was twenty when I set up my software business,' he said. 'Twenty-two when I sold my first licence. I found out where my father lived and went to his house. I figured he'd be proud.' He sighed and rubbed his hands over his face. 'God only knows why. I didn't get beyond the front gate. But I did see a girl swinging in a hammock beneath a tree in the garden.'

Her gaze softened. 'That must have been a shock.'

Shock was an understatement. He'd felt as if a neutron bomb had gone off inside him. 'I'll never forget it,' he said, recalling the power of his reaction as if it were yesterday. 'The sun was shining down on her like she was the chosen one. It was as if she'd been gilded. I couldn't stop staring. Initially in awe and then in growing resentment. It was impossible not to feel envy and rage at the injustice.'

'I'm not sure that anything in that house was gilded.'

'What do you mean?' he asked with a frown.

'You'd have to talk to her.'

His pulse skipped a beat and then began to race. 'I don't think I can.'

'Why not?'

'As I told you before, I don't like rejection.'

'Which is understandable. But Gaby came here to meet you,' Thalia pointed out. 'That's acceptance, not rejection.'

'What if I don't live up to her expectations?' he muttered with an inward wince.

'I'm not sure she has any, but I have her number if you want it.'

He sighed and shifted in the chair, but it did nothing to ease his discomfort. 'I don't know what I want. I don't know how to handle any of this. I was hoping you'd tell me. You're an expert in family dysfunction.'

'Unfortunately, I have no advice,' she said, shaking her head ruefully. 'I've been trying to find a way through my issues for months and have got nowhere, mainly, I suspect, because I'm terrified of discovering that my relationship with my brother has been a lie all these years. I don't think I could bear it if it was. But I know that the situation can't continue. You were wrong about me putting it off because of stubbornness, but you were right about how long it's been dragging on. It probably isn't a very healthy state of affairs, and I guess it is just about possible that Atticus is as unhappy as I am with the way things are. I've yet to find the courage to find out.'

'You and me both.'

'You have a far greater excuse than I do,' she said. 'What you went through must have been deeply traumatic. I'm just a poor little rich girl. There's no need to feel sorry for me. But it's no wonder you have such a problem with privilege. Your father abused it in the worst possible way.'

'My mother made it worse.'

'How?'

'She somehow drilled it into me that we were inadequate,' he said, recalling the many times she'd been let down and poured out her despair and unhappiness to him. 'For years I believed it was my fault that we were where we were. I swore to do better, and I have, materially, but sometimes, deep down, I'm still that angry kid who doesn't feel good enough.'

'None of it was your fault and you're more than good enough.'

Was he? For her? Why was he even thinking about that when on Wednesday she'd be gone? 'She's also the reason I'm still single,' he said, not wanting to think about Thursday and beyond. 'She never got over my father. She died of a broken heart when I was nineteen, which I just couldn't understand when he'd been so cruel. You were right to question my ability to commit. From her, I learned that love is toxic, for the weak, and that with relationships come an imbalance of power.'

'Not always,' she said after a moment's consideration. 'Great examples of love abound. Spend some time with Atticus and Zoe if you need proof. And there wasn't an imbalance of power between us.'

Wasn't there? 'You walked away.'

'Not because I wanted to,' she said. 'Because I had to. For weeks afterwards I felt bereft. I'd thought the world of you. I couldn't eat. I couldn't sleep. Breaking up with you affected me more than I ever thought it would.'

For a second, he could barely breathe. His heart felt too big for his chest. 'Me too,' he confessed gruffly. 'You once claimed I didn't lose my head when we were together, but I did. I thought of you constantly. Whenever we arranged to meet, I used to count down the hours. I saved all the messages you sent and the voicemails you left and still have them. Afterwards, I wanted to call you. I wanted you to call me.'

'What do you think would have happened if we hadn't split up?'

'I don't know.'

But he knew what he'd dreamed of, he knew what deep down he'd craved but hadn't thought he deserved, and it was too much. Too overwhelming and terrifying. He didn't want to talk any more. Or think. Or re-member. He was wrung out. All he wanted right now was to lose himself in her until everything swirling around inside him settled.

'I don't want you to go,' he said, giving free rein to the desire that was beginning to sweep through his body, erasing the memories and the emotions as it did so.

Her gaze darkened and her breath caught. 'All right, I won't.'

'But I don't want to talk any more either.'

'Then what do you want?'

'You.'

It was late when Thalia woke to a disappointingly empty bed, but that was no surprise. She and Santi had talked long into the night. About his life in the Rio favela and hers in the Athens mansion, the differences and the similarities of their upbringings, and about family. When she thought about how hard life had been for him her heart ached. He'd overcome virtually all the odds there were to make a success of himself. With the lawlessness and the violence of his youth, so many where he came from never got that chance.

He was complex, astounding and endlessly compel-ling. She understood him and his need for control so much better now. She felt closer to him than she ever had before, and while that would have alarmed her greatly a week ago, now she was wondering whether it might not be worth pursuing.

According to his revised schedule, she had only another three days here, but she felt it only fair that she offered to extend her stay. She disagreed that they take the day they'd flown out as day one because no work had been done and they'd had quite a few breaks since then. When the one hundred hours were up—and in all honesty she'd rather lost count—maybe they could continue to date. They lived on different continents, and had different demands on their time, but they'd made it work before.

His charity project had a long way to go yet, and she could still self-improve while exploring a new and exciting relationship with a man she was falling hard and fast for. She didn't know why she'd ever believed that those two things were mutually exclusive. She'd made excellent progress in so many areas—Atticus-related issues notwithstanding, although thanks to Santi's support she was going to take the bull by the horns and call him in the next day or two—and she was in a much better place now than she had been thirteen months ago. She was beginning to figure out who she was. Her confidence was returning. She was ready for a proper relationship, with him. The only question was, was he ready for one with her?

Last night's conversations were certainly encouraging. He'd opened up to her in a way that she'd lost all hope of ever experiencing. He'd sought her advice. He'd told her things he admitted he'd never shared with another living soul. They'd connected on a level that went far deeper than anything they'd shared to date.

It thrilled her to know that he'd once been as

equally into her as she'd been into him. Could she begin to hope that was the case now? She was head over heels in love with him, but how did he feel? Last night she'd asked him what he wanted and he'd told her he wanted her. But *how* did he want her? Just physically, or for more?

She would have to tread carefully. The last twenty-four hours had to have been incredibly draining for him and she didn't want to subject him to any more emotional stress. So she would start by drumming up some of that courage she'd mentioned and ask him what he thought of continuing their fling. After all, nothing ventured, nothing gained, and she was ninety-nine percent sure he'd agree. Why wouldn't he? The sex was out of this world. She would keep things light. She would subtly show him he was definitely good enough for her, and try to be good enough for him, and see how things went from there. He'd soon discover that a relationship was nothing to fear. He might even come to learn that love didn't need to be toxic, and when that happened—well, her heart was practically bursting out of her chest just at the thought of it.

But first she had to call Gaby and apologise for last night. She couldn't possibly indulge in giddy dreams about the future when fully deserved guilt was still stabbing at her conscience. So she rolled over, picked up her phone from the bedside table and brought up the number.

'Hi,' she said when her friend answered. 'How are you?'

'Couldn't be better,' said Gaby, who, it sounded, was in a café somewhere. 'How are you?'

Thalia was on cloud nine. She was in love and brimming with excitement about where her relationship with Santi might be heading. But that probably wasn't what Gaby wanted to hear. 'I'm fine,' she said, forcing herself to calm down and focus. 'I just wanted to say again how sorry I am about yesterday evening. I should have listened to you. I made a lot of presumptions that were wholly unfounded. I can't think what came over me.'

'Truly, don't worry about it,' said her very generous-hearted friend. 'How's Santi?'

'OK, I think.'

'What happened after I left?'

'I apologised and we talked. You were right about your father being his.'

There was a brief pause, and then Gaby said wonderingly, 'So he *is* my brother.'

'He is.'

'Will he call me?'

'I think so,' said Thalia, mentally crossing her fingers. 'But maybe not just yet.'

'I can wait. Whenever he's ready. I'm not going anywhere.'

Talking of which… 'Did you get home OK?'

'Not exactly.'

Oh? 'What happened?'

'Nothing,' said Gaby. 'It was just getting late so I decided to spend the night at the hotel.'

Thalia frowned. 'Which hotel?'

'The only one in the area. The Bellavista. I got the last free room.'

What? Her frown deepened. 'That's odd.'

'Why?'

'It's meant to be closed.'

'What for?'

'The fire that happened last weekend,' she said, a strange chill rippling through her. 'I was told it would be shut for a fortnight.'

'It's very much not shut. It doesn't feel as though it ever was. Hang on a moment.' There followed a muffled conversation in Portuguese and then Gaby was back. 'There was no fire,' she said.

'Are you sure?'

'Definitely. Could you have misunderstood?'

It was possible. It wouldn't be the first time. 'Maybe.'

'I'd better get back to breakfast, which, by the way, is excellent.'

'Let's not leave it so long next time. Have a safe trip home.'

'*Adeus.*'

The call ended and Thalia sat up, deeply confused. What was going on? Could Gaby be right? Had she misunderstood the situation at the hotel? She thought back to last Sunday afternoon, following the satnav from the airport, arriving, trying to check in and then being taken into the office where the situation was explained, and... No, she hadn't. She'd been tired and overwrought, and she didn't speak Portuguese, but she'd managed pretty well with a combination of Italian, Spanish and English, and the conversation she'd had with the receptionist had definitely been about a fire in the restaurant.

But why would she have been told there was one when there wasn't? It didn't make sense, although it did explain why she'd felt something was amiss at the time. The cars in the driveway. The absence of any smoke-related evidence. And then, having had no choice but to drive here, pulling up to find Santi already standing in the doorway, as if he and his fully made-up guest suite had been expecting her.

Surely he couldn't have been behind this mysterious fire? she thought, more bewildered than ever. He'd thwarted her every attempt to control the situation she'd found herself in, but to manipulate her like that seemed extreme. Why would he do something of that nature anyway? And what would it mean if, for some unfathomable reason, he *had* been pulling her strings?

There was only one way to find out.

CHAPTER FOURTEEN

DECIDING TO TALK to Thalia had been the best decision he'd ever made, Santi reflected as he pressed some coffee grounds into the filter of a stove-top coffee maker and screwed on the top.

Once he'd started he hadn't been able to stop, and he'd held very little back of the darkness and torment that had consumed him as a teenager.

But she hadn't been put off. She'd been encouraging and sympathetic. She hadn't judged him at any point, even when he told her about the dangerous ways in which he'd channelled his anger—the fights he'd started, the odd jobs he'd done that had taken him onto the wrong side of the law—before finding tranquillity in the soothing logic of coding and problem solving.

Her understanding had loosened the knot of anguish he'd carried with him for so long, and the crushing pressure he'd felt recently was easing. The exposure, the vulnerability and the surrender of power that he'd dreaded had not materialised. On the contrary he felt stronger and more invincible than he ever had before.

She was good for him. In fact, they were good for

each other, and he could no longer remember quite why they'd limited what they were doing to Wednesday. He saw no reason why they shouldn't carry on. He wasn't as hopeless at giving emotional support as he'd always thought. He wanted her more than just physically. He wanted everything she was, for ever. He was head over heels in love with her and it didn't feel toxic at all. It felt thrilling and wonderful. The future—if he could persuade her to be in it—didn't seem nearly as bleak as it once had. Instead, it was full of possibility and hope.

'Good morning,' he said, his heart turning over when she wandered into the kitchen looking both ravished and ravishing, with dishevelled hair, skin that bore the marks of his stubble and the shorts and camisole that made him think of the warm silky softness that he couldn't get enough of.

'It was when I woke up.'

Her tone was unexpectedly cool, and in response to it a sharp flare of alarm leapt in his chest. 'What's happened since then?'

Could she have reflected on everything he'd told her and now be horrified at how screwed up he was? Was she about to tell him she didn't want to have anything more to do with him? The thought of it chilled his blood and drained the strength from his limbs.

'I just spoke to Gaby.'

His vision cleared. The world righted. That was a relief. But why would that turn Thalia's morning from good to bad? 'I thought I might call her later,' he said, in case she was still upset at the way he'd be-

haved towards her friend and his half-sister. 'Intro-
duce myself properly. Explain last night and make an
arrangement to meet.'

'She didn't drive home.'

'Oh?' He set the coffee pot on the stove and lit the
ring beneath it.

'She stayed at the hotel.'

'Well, it's a long way to Ipanema.'

'The one that was supposedly shut for health and
safety reasons following a restaurant fire,' she said.
'Only it turns out there was no fire. It never closed.
But I suspect you already knew that, didn't you?'

Santi stilled. His heart gave a great crash against
his ribs and the air whooshed from his lungs. He'd
forgotten all about the call he'd made and the instruc-
tions he'd issued. So much had happened and changed
since then. He could scarcely believe it had been little
more than a week.

The instinct to defend and deflect—as he'd done
so often before when backed into a corner—sprang
to life. For half a second he considered it, but then he
stamped it out. There was no point in denying what
he'd done when she'd evidently worked out the truth.
He had no defence and he didn't want to lie to her
ever again. 'Yes.'

'How much did it cost you?'

He flinched at the cold accusation he could hear in
her voice. 'A new roof.'

'Why did you do it?'

Why *had* he done it? He must have been mad. He
deserved every inch of her stony expression and the

simmering condemnation that was rolling off her in waves. All he could do was try and explain and hope that in light of everything they'd talked about last night she forgave him.

'I'd planned all along for you to stay here, with me,' he said, willing her to listen to him and give him a chance. 'I didn't appreciate you going off-piste. It was infuriating.'

'So you manipulated the situation. You manipulated me.'

Regret thumped through him, churning up his stomach and tightening his throat. 'I'm sorry,' he said roughly.

'You had no right to do that. I understand your need for control and where it comes from. And I get that you fear chaos ensuing without it. But that's no excuse.'

'I know.'

'What you did makes me question everything else that's happened since Saturday night. It makes me wonder what else you might be manipulating.'

Outwardly, Santi didn't move a muscle. Inwardly, however, every cell of his body was recoiling in icy panic. Under no circumstances must she wonder that. If she got wind of his insane plan for revenge, even though he'd abandoned it days ago, this fledgling relationship of theirs could well lie in ruins.

'I'm not manipulating anything,' he said, his heart pounding so hard it hurt. 'How ever this started, trust what we have now.'

'How on earth can I? And what is that anyway?'

'I don't know,' he had to admit. This was all so new, and he hadn't had a chance to properly figure it out. 'But it's more than just sex.'

Her eyebrows lifted. 'Is it?'

He went cold. His head spun. 'Don't you think so?'

'I did last night,' she said. 'Yesterday—and even this morning—I thought we could see where this went. I thought we had a shot at something great.'

'We do.'

'I'm not so sure now.'

'I screwed up,' he said, feeling as though he was standing on the edge of a giant steep cliff, beneath which lay nothing of the future he'd been tentatively imagining, but instead all of his snarling, snapping fears. 'Forgive me. It won't happen again.'

Thalia wanted to believe Santi. She did understand why he'd done what he'd done and she wished she could make the necessary allowances, brush it aside and move on. But however hard she tried, she couldn't. He'd lied to her. He hadn't given her wishes a second thought before bulldozing them. She'd refused to fall into line and been punished for it. How could she forgive him for that? How could she trust that it was a one-off?

She went through the motions of breakfast and work, struggling to find a way through the chaos in her head, but she couldn't shake the feeling that the sands beneath her feet were shifting. Whereas once she'd thought she had him all figured out, she was now longer certain of anything. He wasn't the man she'd thought he was. The bright, hopeful future she'd dreamed of was now blurry and grey.

The morning dragged by and the sense of unease she felt swelled. She couldn't stop analysing everything else he'd said and done since he'd swooped back into her life, so much of which had bothered her at the time. The determined flirting in the beginning, when at that point their relationship had been purely professional. All that touching on the plane, the innuendo, the knowing smiles, and his subsequent wandering around the house semi-naked. He'd smouldered at her endlessly and had provoked her whenever the opportunity arose. It was as if he'd been trying to seduce her, right from the start, but why would he have suddenly wanted her back in his bed when they'd parted on such bad terms over a year earlier?

On the night of the gala she'd questioned why he had been so determined to secure her services, and that question was now rearing its head again. He could have sought help for his charity endeavours anywhere, and she was good, but so were many others with whom he did not have history. She didn't understand why he'd insisted on bringing her to Brazil when the options she'd presented him with had been perfectly reasonable, even allowing for his need for control. It hadn't been an on-the-spur-of-the-moment sort of a thing. It had been premeditated. He'd even admitted earlier that the plan *all along* had been to have her stay with him.

So just how far back had that plan gone?

How *had* this all started?

And why did she get the feeling that something was still badly wrong?

By lunchtime, Santi couldn't bear the suspicion and wariness with which Thalia kept looking at him any longer. The blood in his veins flowed sluggishly. He was sweating in a way that had nothing to do with the heat of the day. A lead weight had settled on his chest, crushing him with a terrible combination of guilt, remorse, panic and dread.

He could tell that his earlier confession was festering within her. She evidently wasn't able to forgive him as he'd hoped. He was losing her, he sensed with a plummeting stomach. He was falling off that cliff edge and tumbling headlong into the desolation that lay below, and it was every bit as sickening as he'd feared.

He desperately wanted to fix the situation but couldn't figure out the right way to go about it, or even if it was possible. He could give her more time and space but she might never find her way back to him. He could come clean and tell her the truth about everything, but he knew that if he went down that route he risked losing her for good.

However, that was happening anyway, he'd eventually forced himself to acknowledge, cold fingers of fear clawing at his gut as he contemplated the options and their outcomes. And he'd never been any good at passivity. If this relationship stood any chance of survival—and it was too promising to throw away out of cowardice—he had to try and rebuild her trust in him, even if it meant destroying it further first. Even if with the stakes so stratospherically high, the chances of everything he longed for crashing down around him were immense.

He'd faced his demons and survived. Whatever the result of the conversation he had to have with her, however devastating the potential fallout, he'd survive that too. He couldn't do nothing, and he would not go down without a fight.

'Come and sit down,' he said when she returned to the poolside table bearing two tall glasses of fruit juice. 'We need to talk.'

Thalia set the glasses on the table, her hands trembling slightly and her heart thudding way too fast. She thought about the last time that phrase had been uttered—by her, then, though, not him. They'd been over shortly afterwards.

So was that what was going on here? Was Santi going to tell her he'd had a rethink and now wasn't interested in taking their relationship any further? How would she feel if he did? Relieved? Cheated? Or devastated?

Part of her wanted to run away and hide so she didn't have to face whatever it was he wanted to talk about, but that had never solved anything. For *two years* she'd been struggling with her feelings regarding her brother and Zoe mainly by sticking her head in the sand, so she sat down and braced herself.

'First of all,' he said, his expression more serious

than she'd ever seen it before, 'you need to know that I'm in love with you. You are the most incredible woman I've ever met and I want to marry you and spend the rest of my life with you.'

At his unexpected declaration, her heart soared with joy. A tsunami of relief crashed through her. He wasn't putting an end to their affair. Maybe all was not lost. Maybe they could work through her doubts and her worries together.

'I'm in love with you, too,' she said, her voice thick with emotion, 'and I'll marry you any day of the week.'

'Good,' he said, letting out a ragged breath. A light briefly flickered in the dark depths of his eyes before disappearing. 'Remember that.'

'Why?'

'Because you might forget it when you hear what I have to tell you.'

She couldn't imagine forgetting something as momentous as that ever. What could possibly be so bad that she would? 'All right.'

He shoved his hands through his hair and swallowed hard. 'It was no coincidence that I was at the gala on Saturday night.'

Ah. The questions rampaging through her head were finally going to be answered. It was as if he'd read her mind. Again. 'I gathered that,' she said cautiously.

'I always intended to win your lot.'

'I gathered that, too.' She leaned forwards, pulled one of the glasses of guava and pineapple juice towards her and took a sip before setting it back down. 'What I don't understand is why?'

For a moment, Santi didn't respond. Across his face skated a flurry of emotions that she just couldn't identify. Then he took a deep breath and said, 'Revenge.'

She blinked and sat back. 'What?'

'I was out for revenge.'

'On who?'

'You.'

The word hit her like a blow, and for a second she couldn't breathe. She felt as if he'd punched her in the gut. The juice curdled in her stomach. 'Why?'

'Ever since I can remember I've been in control of the relationships I've had,' he said while she fought for composure, for her brain, which had suddenly gone MIA. 'I start them. I finish them. Then you came along and ended ours before I was ready and suddenly I was in control of nothing. You confused the hell out of me. You made me doubt myself for the first time in years and that filled me with anger and resentment, emotions I thought I'd buried long ago. It went on for months, eating me up inside, until I realised I couldn't let it continue. So I came up with a plan.'

Her heart slowed right down. She went very cold. She could never have anticipated this to be his explanation. 'What was it?'

'To take back the power and restore control.'

'How?'

'By seducing you,' he said, his voice cracking, although his steady gaze did not leave hers. 'By getting you to fall for me and then ending it.'

The silence that fell then was thick and deafening. Thalia couldn't speak. She was struggling to process what he was saying. She didn't even know where to start. All she could hear was the thundering of her blood in her ears. 'Was *I* your merger and acquisitions project?'

'Yes,' he admitted gruffly. 'But the night we kissed by the pool, I abandoned it. I realised it was a terrible thing to have done.'

'Because I wasn't complying.'

'You weren't,' he said. 'And that made me reassess. The strength of your will highlighted just how plain wrong I'd been to pursue it. I should never have allowed my insecurities to get the better of me. If I could wind back time and do things differently I would. In a heartbeat. I never expected to fall in love with you again. But I don't think I ever fell *out* of love with you. That was the real reason why I lashed out in Paris. I'd fallen for you—quite possibly the minute I laid eyes on you—and you broke up with me. It wasn't just the rejection that hurt so badly. It was my heart.'

He carried on explaining how he'd felt about her then and how he felt about her now, but to Thalia they were just words, words and more words. All she could think was that this whole thing had just been one big game to him. For her, these last eight days had been a brave leap of faith both professionally and personally. For him, it had been payback for something she hadn't even done.

The relentless flirting and the attention that she'd lapped up now made perfect sense. She'd made it so easy for him. The kisses, the sex, the conversation. She'd shared with him her innermost angst. She hadn't known how right she'd been when she suspected he'd use it against her. She felt like the biggest fool in the history of the world. And the pain of it was so excruciating she had to switch herself off before she burst into tears.

'Say something,' he urged.

'What do you want me to say?' she said numbly, her eyes nevertheless stinging, her throat tight. 'That what you did is OK just because your guilty conscience has forced you to confess? It's very much not OK.'

'I know that. If you let me I'll spend the rest of my life making it up to you. Remember that I love you and you love me.'

Hah. 'I fell in love with a fantasy,' she said bitterly. 'That man doesn't exist.'

'Yes, he does. You're the only person on the planet to know the real me. You've changed me. You've opened my eyes and shown me what love can be. Who I can be with you.'

He reached to take her hand but she whipped it away before he could. 'You've proven yourself to be ruthlessness over and over again, Santi. For all I know, your plan is in full swing, even now, and this is all part of it. You say you love me but how can I believe that? How do I know it's not just a line? How can I ever trust you again?'

'Because I could have got even so many times,' he said, looking and sounding faintly desperate. 'I could have ruined you professionally the minute you revealed what was at stake for you. I could have used our kiss to further my agenda. But I didn't. And it wasn't a conscious decision that I made on either of those occasions. It just never crossed my mind. The truth is I gave up on revenge before I even got going. I love you and I will be sorry for what I tried to do till the day I die.'

Santi stopped, and clearly it was her turn to respond but her head was buzzing. She was sure there was logic to what he said, but she couldn't see it. She still felt so very stupid. So naïve. He'd been right all along about the imbalance of power in a relationship. He'd had it all. She'd had none. But she could redress that. She had some pride left. It was pretty much all she *did* have left.

'I wouldn't worry about it too much,' she said with a brittle smile.

'What do you mean?'

'I've been using you, too.'

He frowned. 'What?'

'Remember the morning I twisted my ankle?'

'Yes.'

'While you were off getting the bandage and the crutches, Atticus rang. He told me Zoe was pregnant. It sent me into a spin. I just wanted to forget that he was drifting even further away from me and, as we both know, you're very good at making that happen.' With effort she mustered up a pitying look. 'You were so easy to seduce. Ironic, now I think about it.'

He paled. He stared at her, as if struck dumb. 'Are you serious?' he managed eventually.

'Why wouldn't I be?'

'I don't believe you.'

Now he knew what it felt like. 'You're not the only one who gets what they want, Santi.' She got up. Her legs were so weak they barely held her up, but they just had to carry her to her room because she couldn't bear to look at him any more. He'd shattered her heart, her hopes and her dreams, and she was on the point of collapse. 'I think we're done here, don't you?'

CHAPTER FIFTEEN

FOR SEVERAL MINUTES after Thalia got up and walked off Santi just sat there, staring at the space she'd occupied, reeling as if she'd physically struck him, the shocking revelation that she'd been using him scything through him and dicing his heart to pieces. Not that he could feel it—he was frozen in shock. Then the shock subsided and in flooded every insecurity he'd ever had, blitzing his brain and battering him on all sides.

Of course she'd been using him, insisted the inferiority complex he'd naïvely assumed that, with her help, he'd conquered. What else could he have expected? He'd been an idiot to think that someone like her would genuinely fall for someone like him. Nothing he did would ever be good enough to impress her.

As he'd always feared, love had made him weak and needy and desperate. He'd handed her his heart and she'd stomped all over it. And as a result he was bleeding as if she'd stabbed him with a thousand knives. He'd all but begged her to believe him, to trust him, but to no avail, and the emotions swirling though him like a hurricane made him want to howl.

He'd taken the biggest risk of his life and he'd lost. So he was glad she was leaving. He was far better off alone. He always had been. Alone, he couldn't be hurt or rejected, and being rid of her was what he'd originally planned. Only he had no power right now, no control. He felt no satisfaction, just a gaping great hole in his chest where she'd been and utter misery.

He'd told her everything. He'd basked in the warmth of her smiles and their conversations. And that had been reciprocated, he was sure. When he thought of all they'd shared, how generous and thoughtful she'd been, how keen she'd been to find out who he was and how she'd let him into her world in return, he couldn't believe that all she'd sought was escape. She'd been as tangled up in him as he had been in her, emotionally as well as physically. No one was that skilled an actor.

So what if with that retaliating shot of hers she'd simply been protecting herself? He could understand that. He'd deployed that defend-and-deflect strategy often enough. She'd been badly bruised by what he'd done. He'd seen it in her eyes and on her face. Why wouldn't she want to cause him as much pain as he'd caused her? Wasn't that exactly what he'd done in Paris?

So what the hell was he doing sitting here pondering the frailty of human nature while she packed up her things? Was he really going to let her walk out of here? If she slipped through his fingers he might never get her back again, and that was something he did *not* want to have to contemplate.

The front door slammed, the sound reverberating through every cell of his being, and he sprang to his feet. This was all wrong. He was in love with her, she was in love with him, and he would make her believe it if it was the last thing he did.

Thalia's eyes stung madly as she threw her suitcase into the boot of the red hired convertible. But she would not let the tears fall. Not until she was back home and on her own. Then she could spend a month crying into her pillow. She knew how this went. She'd done it before. Only this time the pain was so much worse. It was crucifying.

She should never have put him on such a pedestal, she thought heartbrokenly as she climbed into the driver's seat and plugged Rio's main airport into the satnav. He was only ever going to fall off it. No one was flawless. Everyone made mistakes. She could be making one right now. She could be making the biggest mistake of her life...

But no. She wasn't. There was nothing left for her here. Even if she could persuade herself to believe that Santi did love her, that he did regret what he'd done, it was worthless without trust. By destroying that, he'd wrecked anything they might have had.

With a stifled sob, she fired up the engine and was just about to switch the car into gear when the front door flew open. Santi strode out of the house and planted himself an inch in front of the bonnet.

'Stop,' he said, feet wide apart, arms folded over his chest.

Her heart lurched and then began to race. But she'd been distracted by him for the last time. She would never succumb to such lunacy again. 'Move out of the way.'

'No.'

She revved the engine. 'Don't make me run you over.'

His eyes were dark, his expression fierce. 'Do what you need to do, Thalia. I'm staying put.'

And so was she, obviously, because behind her was a wall and, despite everything, she couldn't mow him down. 'What do you want?' she said, taking her foot off the accelerator, killing the engine and glaring at him over the windscreen instead.

'I am not letting you go.'

Her head spun for a second before she hauled it back under control. 'I'm not yours to keep.'

'I love you and you love me. We belong together.'

'You could not be more wrong.'

'We still have work to do.'

'Find someone else. That's what I'm going to do.'

His gaze drilled into hers, so intense, so penetrating, it was as if he was trying to get a glimpse of her very soul. 'Were you really using me?'

She jutted up her chin. 'As much as you were using me.'

'That'll be a no, then, thank God,' he said, his relief visibly immense.

Her strength and fury drained away along with most of her defences. She was tired and sad and trying to figure it all out was so very hard.

'Consider everything we've done together, Thalia. Everything we've talked about, everything we've shared.'

'What do you think I was doing while shoving my things into my suitcase?' she said helplessly. 'I've thought about nothing but that. It didn't work. It only made me more confused.'

'It was all real. Every second of it. You must believe that. You have to trust me.'

'I want to,' she said, her voice raw with the emotion that she simply couldn't hide any more. 'So much. But I can't.'

'You can. Please. I need you.'

It was the crack in his voice and the sheer desperation etched into his features that smashed the last of her weakening defences to pieces, striking her right in the heart. Her chest ached and her vision blurred. Was she *really* going to throw what they had away? Up until this morning, it had been so good. Santi was the only man—her brother aside—who'd ever truly understood her. He had an uncanny ability to read her mind and he'd forced her to confront some difficult truths. He challenged her. He made her laugh. She wanted to spend the rest of her life with him. That hadn't changed.

Perhaps trust was a choice, she thought, her blood pumping faster as the possibility of that hit her. She could choose to believe him when he said he'd given up on his plan for revenge the night they'd kissed by the pool, and that he deeply regretted coming up with the idea in the first place—or she could choose not to believe him. The evidence that their relationship had been genuine was all there. She didn't even have to look very hard. It was in every smile he'd ever given her, every look, every touch.

So maybe what was holding her back from making the choice she desperately wanted to make were *her* insecurities. The fear of it all going wrong again. Of not being enough for him. Of the connection they shared disappearing.

But that was no way to live.

Not when he'd shown her how wonderful the alternative could be.

And why wouldn't she be enough for him? Why would their connection disappear and their relationship implode?

This last year had been all about being brave and taking risks. Was she really going to stop now, at this most crucial moment in her life, when her happiness, her hopes and dreams and her entire future were at stake?

No, she was not. She was going to shake off her doubts and worries and choose to put her faith in him, in them.

'I need you, too,' she said a little giddily, as the gloom and misery lifted to reveal a future that once again looked bright and exciting.

He went very still. His gaze bore into hers. 'What are you saying?'

'That I do believe you and I do trust you. I know you. You know me. Everyone makes mistakes.'

'Not quite like mine.'

'That's true. But I choose to let it go.'

A muscled ticked in his jaw. 'Are you sure?'

'I've never been surer of anything,' she said, her heart beginning to swell. 'I just got a little lost for a while back there.'

'I am sorrier than you will ever know.'

'Enough to come over here and show me how very sorry you are?'

'If I wasn't slightly concerned you might still drive off.'

'Then I will come to you.'

She got out of the car and walked unhesitatingly into his arms. His mouth came down on hers and she lost track of all time and place as he held her tight, as if he couldn't bear to let her go, and kissed her so deeply she didn't ever want to come up for air.

'I love you very much,' she said when they eventually had to break apart.

He smiled and swept her up into his arms. 'I will love you for ever,' he said, and carried her into the house.

EPILOGUE

One year later

AT ELEVEN P.M. on a Saturday night the following September, in the gilded ballroom of a seven-star Rio hotel, the fundraising auction at a gala being held to launch the brand-new Fundação Ferreira was drawing to a close. A sumptuous six-course dinner accompanied by the finest wines had preceded it, and as a result, over the last hour, millions of dollars had been thrown at luxury villas, questionable art and cases of claret, by well-fed, well-oiled guests determined to outdo each other.

Santi lounged at a table in the centre of the room and reflected that the last time he'd attended a charity auction, he'd wound up acquiring a wife. Tonight, however, he was not bidding on any of the lots. Tonight, he was celebrating the culmination of many months of hard work.

He truly did not think he could be happier or prouder of everything he and Thalia had achieved in the past twelve months. They divided their time between Greece and Brazil. Her business was flourishing. The charities he'd set up beneath the umbrella of his foundation were already changing lives in the favelas.

Perhaps most importantly, the sibling troubles that had caused them both so much grief were history. His relationship with Gaby, tentative at first, had gone from strength to strength. Thalia and Atticus had talked and reshaped their thirty-two-year twinship. They were all here tonight, in fact. Atticus and Zoe were across the table. On his left was his sister and to his right was the woman with whom he was more in love with every day that passed.

'You did it,' she murmured, her eyes shining with warmth, love and pride as the gavel came down on the last lot and the band struck up a tune.

'*We* did it,' he replied, resting a protective hand on her seven-month bump and feeling their baby kick.

'Want to dance?'

'Always.'

* * * * *

HARLEQUIN
Reader Service

Enjoyed your book?

Try the perfect subscription for Romance readers and get more great books like this delivered right to your door.

See why over 10+ million readers have tried Harlequin Reader Service.

Start with a Free Welcome Collection with free books and a gift—valued over $20.

Choose any series in print or ebook. See website for details and order today:

TryReaderService.com/subscriptions

persuasion his-arguable and-put..........
hee was not. she said.